I0589869

SCOUTS & SCALAWAGS

Growing Up in the City of Saints

Growing Up in the City of Saints

is a two-part American adventure series

written by Dennis Ganahl

Scouts & Scalawags Growing Up in the City of Saints, 2021

Heroes & Hooligans Growing Up in the City of Saints, 2017

SCOUTS & SCALAWAGS

Growing Up in the City of Saints

Text copyright © 2021 by Dennis Ganahl

All rights reserved. No part of this publication may be produced, distributed or transmitted in any form or by any means, including photocopying, recording, or other electronic or mechanical methods, without the prior written permission of the publisher, except in the case of brief quotations embodied in critical reviews and certain other noncommercial uses permitted by copyright law. For permission requests, write to the author.

Ingram ISBN 978-1-0879-6122-4

Any references to historical events, real people, or real places are used fictitiously. Names, characters, and places are products of the author's imagination and storytelling.

Front cover image by Dennis Ganahl and Ryan Morris

Book graphic design by Ryan Morris

Distributed by IngramSpark

First Edition printing, 2021

Published by Grey Matter, LLC

St. Louis, MO

DEDICATION

I dedicate this book to everyone who has encouraged me to write especially my dear wife, Dr. Gina Ganahl, and my sons Kevin and Denny. My long list of encouraging patrons includes many longtime friends from grade school, high school and college. It also includes the nuns who tediously taught me spelling, verb tenses, grammar and how to diagram a sentence on the chalkboard. Their dedication to pounding the finer points of the English language into our thick know-it-all heads was transformative. I remember one poor soul. His Brylcream soaked through to page 96 of his spelling book while it balanced precariously on his head. He was kneeling in front of the class for clowning around. Each time it slid off; time was added. I also include my high school teachers who worked tirelessly to keep our minds off girls and sports and in our books. Finally, to my college professors who insisted good grammar was always appropriate and that great literature improved my quality of life.

Last, and most importantly, I want to thank the titanium-willed women who shaped my life. It's not easy to manage and direct an iron-willed young man. It takes titanium and love. I've been very blessed to have the best grandmother, Ruth Marie Carmichael-Strub, and mother, Doris Irene Strub-Ganahl possible.

I thank all of you for helping me become the best man and writer I can become. I hope you enjoy my second novel more than my first.

Grateful,

Dennis

ACKNOWLEDGMENTS

I want to acknowledge the people who were always there for me. Besides the daily support provided by my wonderful family, it took a city of saints to support me and make my life meaningful.

I want to thank everyone who reads my books and my friends who always laughed and had fun with me. I enjoy writing and publishing books. It requires lots of knowledge and skills that people have taught me at the St. Louis Writers Guild and the St. Louis Publishers Association.

My St. Kevin grade school teachers especially Sister Lois Ann and Sister Mary Karen worked like bees to teach me the fundamentals of reading, writing and arithmetic. At William Cullen McBride High School, teachers like Reverend Paul Ryan, Reverend John Rechtien, Michael Flott, Robert Fania, Dr. Raymond Breun and Tom Smith dedicated their lives to my education. Richard Erickson, Dale Gaston, Frank Dobyns and Tom Ladwig were my favorite college professors. They taught my brother and me how to publish a newspaper, hence, a book. I also want to thank my older brother Dr. Richard J. Ganahl III. He provided me with unerring examples of how to be a best friend and a big brother.

Besides Dad, I've had many strong men in my life. Jim Graffigna, my youth baseball coach, and John "Jack" Roberson, my youth basketball coach, were great motivators and both graduated from McBride. John Hunt, Don Martini and Jim Patterson changed my suburban life into an outdoor adventure based on self-reliance and preparedness when they led Troop 643 and me to honor.

I want to directly thank the people who help me publish my books. Ryan Morris is a very patient and talented graphic artist. Dena Hull, Craig Niehaus, Kevin Cundiff, and Alisa Correa have supported me by reading my not-ready-for -primetime beta drafts and by giving me valuable feedback and support. David Peters, author, artist and scholar is always generous with his ideas and support.

CONTENTS

PREFACE

Everyone has at least one good story to tell, and they're happy to tell it. Just ask. My story is the *Growing Up in the City of Saints* books. They're books about a rare and romantic place in American history. It's a place and a time where people didn't always lock their cars or their homes. The kids had the freedom to ride their bikes wherever they wanted, and their parents didn't always know where they were. Kids didn't have virtual friends and digital chats. They ran the streets, played in the fields and rarely spoke on the phone in case they'd be overheard. It was a time when families and churches were the center of their lives, but the times changed.

These novels tell the story of a boy named Mickey growing out of his age of innocence. He's growing up during a time when freedom came with personal responsibility and sin was avoided. It was a time when everyone tried their hardest and only winners got trophies. It was a time when love was given unconditionally, but trust had to be earned. Mickey and his friends were growing up in the City of Saints, and they were all expected to live like one.

Listen to these Rock 'n Roll music stations while you read this book.

Everyone uses their favorite songs to create personal music soundtracks throughout their lives. I created two free Spotify music stations that I suggest you listen to while you read my books. These stations were created to imitate the music being played on Pop AM music stations like St. Louis' KXOK and its favorite DJ, Johnny Rabbitt. *Heroes & Hooligans* and *Scouts & Scalawags Growing Up in the City of Saints* are books about kids growing up in 1963. Besides hanging out with friends, nothing was more important than the Rock 'n Roll music blaring from their cars, their transistor radios, and of course, mom and dad's stereo console. Rock 'n Roll was their soundtrack, and its artists were their cultural icons. In 1963, Pop music was transitioning from Elvis to the 4/4 beat of the shaggy-haired Beatles.

The Beatles' British Invasion made them the new maestros of the American music scene. I wrote *Scouts & Scalawags* to reflect that fact. The chapters' titles are the names of Beatle songs. Beatles' songs became the memory-milestones of found and lost loves, and they reflected the social revolutions for civil rights, war protests and rebellion.

These two stations will help you remember something you did or someone you knew in 1963. These Spotify stations play the top music, commercials and TV program theme songs from 1963.

They are based on my research of the music being played at that time. The stations can be found under the titles *Growing Up in the City of Saints*, and *Scouts and Scalawags Christmas Playlist*. I encourage my readers to listen to these stations while they read to set the mood, and conjure up memories. Play the *Growing Up in the City of Saints* playlist for both *Heroes & Hooligans* and *Scouts & Scalawags*. The Christmas playlist is meant for the last five chapters in *Scouts & Scalawags*. The Beatle music I included are the songs they released in 1963, and the songs that I used for chapter titles.

BOOK COVER

The *Scouts & Scalawags'* book cover is a montage of 1963 cultural icons. They include rich symbolism which focuses on Norman Rockwell's painting of a Boy Scout featured on the 1963 BSA Handbook. The scout is wearing George Harrison's Sgt. Pepper's feathered tricorn, and he's carrying the Beatles' second American album released on January 20, 1964. The scout is crossing Abbey Road.

ಌ

I SHOULD'VE KNOWN BETTER

I felt like a grown-up walking along the gravel shoulder of the two-lane St. Charles Rock Road. I was fingering the money in the front pocket of my cutoff blue jean shorts. To avoid the monotony of the walk, every once in a while, I'd stop to see if I could magically transport myself to the doorway of Tino's Barber Shop. No matter how hard I concentrated on vaporizing myself, it didn't work. It was frustrating, but I kept trying. I smiled as I passed Jumping Jack City because it had made this moment possible.

In just a few short weeks of working at Jumping Jack City, I had made enough money to pay for my first barbershop haircut. It was going to cost me one dollar. Jumping Jack City had 18 trampolines packed with kids and their families all the time. Many of the dads and some of the kids had sprained their backs on the trampolines. Moms were smart enough not to jump. My friends and I hung out there in the evenings because the older kids hung out there. The trampolines were set over large holes dug as deep as a grave in the ground. No one could fall off the trampolines. They were ground high. People just landed on the gravel, or they got their legs and arms entangled in the large chrome metal springs hooked to the trampolines.

I discovered my pot of gold one Saturday morning when I went there to jump. I only had a quarter so the owner would only let me jump 15 minutes. It was usually a dollar an hour, but nobody was there that morning. As I was taking off my well-worn, end-of-summer, before-I-get-my-new-Keds-for-fall shoes to jump, I saw two things. The first was a lot of trash, like empty cups, napkins, and hamburger bags in the dirt pit under my trampoline. The second thing I saw took my breath away. It was a crinkled up one-dollar bill mixed in with all of the trash. My eyes grew to the size of silver dollars when I saw it. For me to get a dollar, I had to cut and trim the grass on somebody's yard or shovel the snow off their driveway, porch, and sidewalks. The dollar greenback laying in the pit looked like easy money to me.

I stole a glance towards the owner's booth. When I didn't see the owner, I scrambled between the giant springs like a rat after cheese down into the dirt pit. There, I snatched that dollar bill and stuffed it into the same shorts I was wearing today and scrambled up as quickly as I could. When I got to the top of the trampoline, the owner was standing there staring down at me.

He looked like a typical mad dad with his hands on his hips and his lips pursed like he was snarling.

"What the heck are you doing kid? You're not supposed to be down there. You could've gotten hurt," he exclaimed as he pointed into the dark pit.

"Nothing," I said, trying to think of an excuse and look like a repentant sinner. My brain cells were firing up like a Fourth of July fireworks display. I'm sure I looked as guilty as someone who just stole money out of the collection basket at church.

"I couldn't believe all of that trash down there. So, I climbed down to see how much there was," I fibbed, trying to flip the guilt back at him while I pointed into the pit mimicking him.

"Yeah, I know. It looks pretty crummy down there. Doesn't it?" He apologized, looking more repentant than me. If you're born in my Catholic neighborhood, you're taught to feel guilty even if you just did something neighborly for someone.

"I'm just too big to climb between those springs and get all of the litter out," he sighed looking down into the pit.

Litter had become a new word for me over the summer because of the large metal can sitting next to the Rexall Drug store. The 50-gallon metal drum was painted white. It had a sign painted on its side that said, "Don't be a litterbug," with a painting of a yellow and black insect that looked like a giant bumblebee.

The guys and I regularly checked the litter can for bottles with a two-cent deposit ever since they put it outside Rexall's front door. Before the can was there, people put their bottles and trash any place they dropped them.

Before the litterbug can, people threw their trash down wherever they were when they finished eating, drinking or reading. Many people didn't think to take their trash home to throw it away.

Litter lined our roads and alleys. It wasn't unusual to see people drive down the Rock Road or any street for that matter and flip their wadded-up Chuck-A-Burger, Henry Hamburger or Burger Bar sacks, which were full of paper wrappings and leftover hamburgers and fries, out their car windows. When the bags of trash hit the pavement at 30 miles per hour, they busted wide open, and the garbage flew all over the roadway. Paper cups exploding into ice, straws and plastic cup tops quickly followed the bursting bags of flying trash. When cars stopped for red traffic lights, men and women, young and old, opened their car doors or rolled down their windows and dumped ashtrays full of stinky cigarette butts or anything else they didn't want in their cars on the road too. Litterbugs didn't pay any mind to how their litter looked lying in the road as they drove away. After they dropped their litter, it was somebody else's problem. I guessed it was the same story at Jumping Jack City.

Without really thinking it through, I said, "I can fit between those springs, mister. I'll pick the litter up for you. It'll sure look a lot better when it's not down there," I said, giving him my best church kid to parent smile.

Thoughtfully rubbing his chin like a fishmonger and squinting his eyes until they were almost closed he asked, "How much do you want to be paid, kid? I'm not rich, you know."

It was my turn to stroke my chin and squint my eyes. I had to be careful not to demand too much or ask too little. I could tell this guy was going to be a tough nut to crack. He looked so tight he probably squeaked when he walked. Now, that he had the idea I figured he'd get bids from other desperate kids if I was too expensive.

"Oh, not much," I hemmed, quickly estimating the money that might be hidden in the litter. "How about I come here twice a week? You can give me twice the amount of free jump time it takes for me to clean out the pits, and give me a soda of my choice from your soda machine."

"It's a deal," he proclaimed, and then he shook my hand so roughly my eyes rolled and my teeth rattled.

"I'll start right now if you'll give me my quarter back?" I replied.

"Done," he said. "Get to work. Oh, by the way, what's your name, kid?"

"My name's Mickey McBride," I said, "What's yours?"

"People call me Big Ben," he said over his shoulder as he squeaked away towards his office proud as a peacock of the deal he'd just made.

Before Big Ben knew it all of the pits were clean, and I had two dollars and 85 cents in my pocket. I chose a bottle of orange Whistle soda just like Texas Bruce huckstered on the Wrangler Club TV show to drink.

Litter was strewn all along the used car lots lining the Rock Road as I approached Tino's Barbershop. Tino had a cool black antique Ford sitting out front of his shop. It had a hand-painted barbershop sign on its rear spare tire. His red, white and blue barbershop pole was spinning next to his front door.

Tino's was always busy. Old and young men of all shapes and sizes were continually walking in and out all day long. There weren't many kids. It looked like a happening kind of place as bus drivers, laborers, insurance and real estate salesmen, office workers and grandpas paraded in and out every day except Sundays and Mondays.

I'd been rehearsing what I was going to tell Tino for the past couple of days when he asked me what kind of haircut I wanted. Dad had cut my hair my whole life, and we had argued every time he cut it. Nothing ever changed; it was always the same routine.

He'd ask me how I wanted my hair cut, and then I'd tell him. Then Dad would cut it the way he wanted it—in a Princeton. A Princeton was a short haircut all over, just like a crew cut, except for a little tuft of hair in the front. It was left just long enough to comb it up and a little to the side. After Dad would cut my hair, I'd look in the mirror and get angry. Then Dad would say, "You look good in a Princeton, Mickey. You look athletic and smart." I hate how my hair looks after Dad cuts it.

At the end of our argument, Dad would say, "Look, when I cut your hair you're getting a Princeton. When you have enough money Mr. Smarty Pants Rockefeller, go to a barbershop. Pay him to cut your hair the way you want it. You look good. Quit arguing." Then we each stormed away mad. It happened every month of my life ever since I could remember.

To get my hair cut today, I hadn't gotten haircuts for the last two months to grow my hair longer. Dad was grumpy so I had to get it cut. Long hair had become popular ever since Elvis hit the music scene sporting his iconic greasy pompadour.

Personally, I liked President Kennedy's hairstyle. Most Catholic boys did. He had longer hair than most of our fathers, and it wasn't greasy. It was so dry; it blew in the wind. His hairstyle was cool. Our Catholic fathers couldn't say we couldn't get our hair cut like President Kennedy's, and our moms loved our debonair president's hair style.

What Mom and Dad didn't know was I saw a record album of a band from England called the Beatles at Tommy's house last week. It was Tommy's older sister's album. Its title was "Introducing the Beatles England's No. 1 Vocal Group." There was a color photo of the four guys on the cover. The Beatles' hairstyles were even cooler than President Kennedy's. Their hair was longer and shaggier and precisely how I wanted my hair to look. I wanted Tino to give me a Beatle cut. Then, I'd tell my parents I got a Kennedy haircut. They'll never know the difference because they don't know about the Beatles.

Dad won't leave my hair long because he said it makes me look like a girl, and that it won't look good with a baseball cap. He said, "You'll really look just like a Suzie with long hair, Mickey."

I didn't care. Everybody already called me Suzie anyway because Suzie's Brand Tomatoes was the sponsor of our baseball team. Now, I've got my own money, and I am going to get my hair cut just like I want it cut. I want a Beatle cut for the first day of school. So, that's what I am doing with the money in my pocket.

I felt like a grown-up going to Tino's Barber Shop with my own money jingling in my pocket. I was even going to give a silver quarter tip to Tino after he gave me my Beatle cut.

I didn't know what to expect inside a barbershop because I've never been in one, and curtains covered its windows. As I turned the handle and pushed open the heavy wooden door, an overhead bell rang 'ding-a-ling,' and the outside sunlight flooded the inside of the dark shop. A bluish-grey cloud of cigarette smoke hit me smack in the face and escaped out the doorway. Pungent smells of stale cigarette smoke, Old Spice after-shave and other manly scents like sweat, newspaper and dirt filled my nostrils and made me cough. I paused.

For a moment, there was total quiet. All I could hear was the tinny sound of the Cardinals' game on the radio. Suddenly, a man's voice brusquely yelled, "You're letting the air conditioning out, kid. Close the door."

Quickly, I stepped inside the men's world and nervously pulled the door closed behind me. The bell above the door rang 'ding-a-ling,' again. After the bright sunlight, it looked like a cave inside. After some quick eye blinks to help me focus, my eyes started dripping like water faucets because of the thick cumulus cloud of cigarette smoke.

Then, a more friendly voice said, "Please take a number, young man. We'll get to you as soon as we can."

I shook the tears from my eyes, and grabbed a piece of white metal with a black number '6' painted on it. Six was my favorite number because it was Stan Musial's number. I felt lucky and lost at the same time. None of the men were looking at me. They were sitting in chairs that surrounded the shop. Most had their backs turned to me. They were facing each other to tell jokes, slap their knees and laugh out loud while they blew smoke into each other's faces. Tino's reminded me of our clubhouse except we didn't smoke.

As I became oriented to the cacophony of manly sights, sounds and smells in the dim light, I saw three barbers' chairs. Each barber chair had a man sitting in it, but it looked like barbers were sitting in two of them talking with everybody else. Each of the barbers wore a white barber's jacket with a comb in its front pocket. The barber chair closest to the front door had a man getting his haircut. That barber said, "Hello, I'm Tino. Take a seat, and we'll call your number when it's your turn." His calm voice was the one that had told me to take my number.

None of the men or chairs in the shop looked alike. They were dressed like they were at work. Some had taken off their sport coat and tie and some were dressed in blue jeans and work boots. None of them wore shorts or t-shirts even though it was still summer-hot outside. Some of the chairs were for kitchens, some were for offices, some were wooden, some were chrome, some were steel, some had leather pads, some had thick vinyl upholstery and others didn't have any padding. Luckily, the window air-conditioner which had ribbons fluttering from it, was barely blowing cool stinky air around the shop. Without it, everyone would've had even larger sweat stains in the armpits of their shirts. I couldn't count how many men were there to figure out how long of a wait I had. It was comforting to hear Harry Caray calling the Cardinal game on the shop's radio.

Gingerly, I stepped around all of the men and said, "Excuse me, sir," to everyone as I scuttled around the shop to find someplace to sit. The only place was a footstool in the very back corner of the shop next to a rack of tattered magazines. There were lots of old *Look, Life, Time, Saturday Evening Post and Sports Illustrated* magazines. There weren't any comic books.

The only magazine that wasn't at least three years old was a *Life* magazine. It had a photograph of Sandy Koufax tipping his Dodgers cap on the cover. Sadly, the Dodgers were in first place, and my beloved Cardinals were in second. It made me sad to think about it. Mindlessly paging through the magazine, I heard Harry Caray say something that broke my heart. He said, almost in tears, that Stan Musial was going to retire at the end of the season. I couldn't believe what I heard. Was it true?

As I replayed it in my mind and thought through all of the meanings and nuances, I felt panicked. My brain went numb like I had just eaten a Popsicle too fast. I was shocked and sad all at the same time. It felt like someone I knew had just died. I was hoping it was a cruel joke by Harry Caray.

I sat in mute silence, as my mind whirled over the sad possibilities. Then the barbershop bell rang 'ding-a-ling' and bright sunlight flooded inside as another cloud of smoke escaped outside.

My red, swollen and watering eyeballs readjusted to the bright sunlight as a tall black silhouette, that looked like Elvis, stepped inside. Everyone, but Harry Caray, went silent as the stranger slowly sauntered and kind of wiggled inside. When he closed the door, the bell rang 'ding-a-ling.'

As the silhouette stepped into the dim light of the shop, I saw a man wearing a tight white t-shirt, tight blue jeans, black leather belt, black boots and a humongous black pompadour, but something looked out of place. The guy's pompadour wasn't greasy like Elvis'. It was puffy like a woman's beehive hairdo. He had a lit cigarette dangling from his lower lip; he looked like he was pouting as a halo of smoke encircled his head.

Everyone glared at him impatiently, as he loudly said, "Hey Daddy-O! Waiting makes me all jittery. I need a haircut right now. I've got places to go and fans to meet."

Before Tino could answer, the Elvis-wannabe whipped out a can of Alberta VO5 hairspray, popped off the plastic top, and wildly sprayed a large cloud of aerosol hairspray over his pompadour. Seeing the fog of hairspray mix with the halo of smoke around his head reminded me of when we rode our bikes behind the mosquito fog truck that sprayed our neighborhoods.

Life happens fast. We all see things like people slipping and falling on an ice patch that we wish we could see again. We want to turn back the hands of time to re-watch something in slow motion over and over to savor each Nano-second. I want to save those moments to show my friends later again and again. Wouldn't it had been cool if our TVs could do that when we're watching a Cardinals' baseball game? Imagine. We could magically stop time. I would've stopped it when the cranky old man in church scolded Donnie and me right before he sat on his Homburg hat and crushed it. That was hilarious. We couldn't stop snickering at him as he tried to push it back into shape. We finally left church so we wouldn't get in trouble. I'd like to see that again.

This was one of those moments. Something happens so quickly you can't fathom what happens much less understand how it happens. Your mouth goes whomper-jawed. Your eyes open so wide you're afraid your eyeballs are going to fall out because you're not blinking. Those moments were impossible to believe.

As we stared at the Elvis look-alike with his dangling cigarette, he saturated his pompadour with hairspray. Instantaneously, his hair ignited into a rainbow-colored fireball of neon orange, yellow, blue and white flashes. The rainbow burst lasted only as long as a camera's flashbulb. In a split-second, the fluorescent flash had vanished. The only thing left was his smoldering head—without any hair. His black cotton candy pompadour became a puff of smoke that magically kept the shape of his former pompadour, but only for a moment. It was an astonishing scene that was burned into my brain.

Then, as if nothing happened, a barber said nonchalantly, "Number six. It's your turn." Didn't he just see Elvis' hair catch fire and go up in a rainbow puff of smoke? It wasn't a hallucination.

I couldn't concentrate. For a moment, I couldn't even remember where I was or what I was supposed to do or say. I felt lost and confused. Then I heard a solemn voice ask again, "Number six, are you awake? It's time to get your goldilocks cut off. Please step on up number six."

Nobody said a word or tried to help Elvis. Then, he mumbled something incoherently and wanly waved good-bye. Very un-coolly, he stumbled and kind of staggered out of the barbershop. He was stunned and confused by what had just happened. As he pulled the door closed, its bell rang 'ding-a-ling.'

The moment the door closed everyone, except Tino and me, collapsed into laughter. The noise was so loud and raucous the men looked crazed or like they had rabies. They were slapping their knees, and each other, on their shoulders and backs like Stan the Man had just hit a winning home run. Some fell to their knees and were crawling around on the floor like babies laughing. One of the guys rolled over onto his back and was kicking his legs into the air. Tears flowed down his cheeks and puddled on the floor. Almost everyone held their stomachs and laughed like hyenas pointing to the spot where the man's hair flashed into an iridescent cloud.

Everyone, except Tino and me, was laughing so hard their faces turned as red as beets. Most broke into a sweat. They were drooling and their eyes were as bloodshot as mine were from the cigarette smoke. The sickening smell of his burnt hair made me gag.

I was afraid to walk to the barber's chair because of the men rolling on the floor.

As the noise quieted to a low roar, the same brusque voice I heard when I entered said, "Hey kid, it's your turn. You have to sit in that chair," as he pointed to the barber's chair. Everyone started laughing again except me. Tino smiled.

Still in shock, I trudged up to the middle barber's chair and nervously sat in its plush leather seat. "Does he need the kiddy booster, Lorenzo?" the brusque voice snorted as everybody laughed.

"No, he's tall enough Bert," chuckled Lorenzo. "He's just shocked about that guy's hair catching fire and Stan Musial retiring that's all. Are you alright, kid? How do you want your hair cut?"

Sitting in the barber's chair, instead of our kitchen chair, left me feeling stressed. Would my hair explode? What was I supposed to do with all of my Musial baseball cards? Should I trade them or keep them? Scared and disappointed, I wanted to cry but I couldn't. I was in a barbershop full of crazed men looking at me like they expected my head to burst into flames. I closed my eyes tightly, and tried to gather my thoughts.

Then, Lorenzo said, "Come on, kid, time is money. How do you want me to cut your hair?" Focusing, I tried to pull myself together and stammered, "I want you to cut my hair to look like President Kennedy's but keep it a little bit longer, please?" I asked more than demanded.

"Sure, I can do that," Lorenzo assured me. Then he snapped a blue and white striped sheet on the side of his chair, swept it around the front of me and fastened it behind my neck all in one smooth motion. Softly, he ran his long black comb through my windblown hair. I had grown my hair out for this first-time-ever professional barbershop haircut. I wanted to be the only kid at St. Kevin Grade School with a Beatle cut on the first day of school.

As Lorenzo continued to comb my hair, I took a deep breath, exhaled slowly and kept my eyes shut tight. I didn't want to look at the men still laughing and cutting up. The smells and the sounds of the barbershop quickly faded away as I fell soundly asleep.

Mom told me, when I was a baby she would play with my hair to put me to sleep. The same thing happened to me when Dad cut my hair. I'd fall asleep and wake up with my hair cut. It was amazing. I never knew what had happened because I slept so deeply.

So, I wasn't surprised when Lorenzo shook my shoulder and whispered in my ear, "Wake up. I'm finished." I remember shaking my head and saying, "What? Huh?"

I had trouble getting oriented as to where I was and what had happened. Then, I remembered everything that had happened and got very excited about my Beatle haircut. My heart was pumping like a bunny rabbit's, when Lorenzo handed me a mirror as big as my face, smiled and said, "How do you like it?"

My heart soared as I focused on my face in the mirror, but I became confused. It looked like Lorenzo had cut my hair into a Princeton not a Beatle cut. I blinked my bloodshot eyes in disbelief. Was my hair longer than it looked or did Lorenzo cut my hair short like Dad did?

"Sir, I thought I told you I wanted my hair cut like President Kennedy's just a little longer," I said respectfully.

"Yes, you did. Then you fell asleep. I couldn't ask you any questions. Tom over there said you're a baseball player and you needed your hair cut short for baseball. So, I cut it into a Princeton. It looks terrific. Don't you like it?" Then, Lorenzo looked pleadingly into my eyes willing me to like my haircut.

I was numb. I didn't know what to say. I hated my haircut but Lorenzo looked so sad. The man with the brusque voice said, "Your haircut looks good, kid. You don't want to look like a sissy-girl, do you?"

"Heck no," I lied thinking the Beatles didn't look like girls. "I like my haircut, thank you, sir," I said as I angrily climbed out of the chair and dug into my shorts to get my dollar bill to pay him.

Inside, my soul was on fire. I wanted to scream as loud as I could, "YOU DIDN'T GIVE ME MY BEATLE CUT, YOU BIG JERK! NOW I'M NOT GOING TO HAVE A BEATLE CUT FOR THE FIRST DAY OF SCHOOL. MY DAD WOULD'VE CUT MY HAIR LIKE THIS FOR FREE. GUESS WHO'S NOT GETTING A SILVER QUARTER TIP?"

Instead, I smiled courteously and was furious at myself for not speaking up. Just like I had been taught.

As I left Tino's barbershop, I closed the door harder than I should've and the bell rang 'ding-a-ling.' Then, I heard the men start laughing again.

What started out to be a fantastic day turned into a stinky rotten day. Everything was going terribly. Stan the Man was retiring, and I just paid the barber a dollar to scalp me. Lorenzo took my hard-earned money to cut my hair the way he wanted. I started to cry as I ran to find the best Cardinals' fan I knew, my grown-up friend, Bob.

Bob was the African-American custodian at the Kroger's store. If I was right, he was listening to the last couple of innings of the Cardinals' game while he worked on the dock. I wanted to ask him what he thought about Stan the Man retiring at the end of the season. When I got to the loading dock, he was sitting next to his white plastic Sears & Roebuck Silvertone radio. Usually, Bob worked while he listened to the games. It was strange to see him sitting next to his radio with his ear close to the speaker as if he couldn't hear it well.

Relieved to see him, I jumped up on the dock and yelled, "Hey, Bob." I was hoping to find some sympathy and understanding.

Surprised to see me, Bob quickly put his forefinger to his lips indicating for me to stay quiet. He kept his ear close to the radio's speaker, so he didn't miss a single syllable of what was being said. He looked more serious than I had ever seen him. I crept up to him like a mouse so I could hear too. I figured something had happened to a Cardinal player or there was a close play at the plate.

The man's voice on the radio sounded rich and deep like a priest or somebody important. Then the voice said, "Free at last! Free at last! Thank God Almighty, we're free at last!"

After the man on the radio said those words, it sounded like clapping and applause was coming from the small plastic radio. Wondering what was happening, I looked more closely at my friend, Bob. He was sitting on the wooden peach crate he used as a chair to eat his lunch. He was crying just as I had been. I knew Bob would be sad about Musial but I didn't realize how sad.

I fidgeted because I felt awkward sitting there. I watched as my friend wiped tears from his eyes with his large strong hands. A few tears escaped and rolled down his cheek onto his white shirt. Slowly, he turned towards me and turned off his radio. Bob looked happy but he was crying. I had only seen one man cry before. Dad cried the day his father died.

"Are you crying about Stan Musial retiring at the end of the season, Bob?" I asked innocently, "I cried."

"No, Mr. Mickey. That makes me sad but not sad enough to cry," said Bob, as he lightly chuckled, sniffed and looked me in the eyes. "Besides, I'm not crying because I'm sad. I'm crying because what the Reverend Martin Luther King just said makes me happy."

"You're happy, Bob? Mom cries about happy things sometimes. I was crying when I heard about Stan the Man in the barbershop. It makes me sad to think about him not being with the Cardinals anymore. What're we going to do without Stan the Man, Bob?"

"I'm not sure, but we'll manage. You got a nice haircut, Mr. Mickey. Your hair was looking raggedy. Did you get it cut for school next week?"

"Yeah, but I wanted a Beatle cut, and the barber scalped me when I fell asleep in the chair. It makes me mad. I had to pay him anyhow but I didn't give him a tip. I'm never going back there ever again. Hey Bob, if you aren't crying about Stan Musial what are you crying about?"

"Well, I believe my family's life is about to get a lot better because things are going to be a lot fairer here in the good ol' USA."

"What kind of things, Bob?"

"Things you wouldn't know much about, Mr. Mickey. You're too young."

"I'm not a kid anymore, Bob. I just paid for my haircut. Didn't I? I'm grown up."

"Yes, you did and I'm very proud of you for working hard enough to make your own money. You're a good worker, and you're growing into a good man."

"Well, what did that man say that made you so happy, Bob?"

"Lots of things, Mickey. You see people with brown skin like mine don't get to do certain things other people with skin-colored white like yours get to do. That makes me sad but things are going to change and get better."

"What can't you do, Bob? You can do everything I can do, except you're not as fast as me. That's all."

"Oh, I don't get to do certain things Mr. Mickey because I have brown skin. My sons, Donald and Keith, who are your age, can't go to any school they want. And I can't buy a home anywhere I want to buy a home. Some people won't let me drink out of every water fountain, stay in some hotels and eat at certain restaurants just because of my skin. Even Jackie Robinson couldn't stay with the white players on the Dodgers in the hotels. It's just not fair, and that's all there is to say about it," he said as he slapped his knee for emphasis.

"You're right Bob, that's not fair but I thought you had a home already."

"Oh, I do. When I got this job at Kroger, we moved out of the Pruitt-Igoe housing project. Then I bought a home on Highland Avenue in Wellston but people wouldn't want me to buy a home here in St. Ann because of the color of my skin, Mr. Mickey."

My head was spinning. I didn't understand what Bob was talking about. I didn't know about these kinds of things.

"Everybody here at the store likes you, Bob. I'd love for you to live next to me. We're best friends. My parents wouldn't care. Then, Donald and Keith can play with all of my friends and me. It'd be great!"

"I know we'd have a grand time together, Mr. Mickey," and he gave me a peaceful smile and gently squeezed my shoulder.

I didn't understand all of the things that made Bob sad but it didn't matter. Bob was my friend, and I was worried he was sad. I forgot all about my haircut and Stan Musial. They were not that important to me anymore. Bob's feelings were a lot more important. We sat on our peach crates quietly staring off into space for a little while. I was trying to understand the things Bob had said, and decided to talk to Mom and Dad about it at dinner.

Finally, Bob slapped his thighs with his calloused hands, stood up, stretched and said, "Well, I better get back to work, Mr. Mickey."

"Yeah, I better get going too. Mom is taking me to buy school supplies. Great seeing you, Bob."

We waved goodbye. I scratched my freshly mowed head wishing it was a Beatle cut, and was thinking there was a lot more to being an adult than making money as I walked home.

❧

GETTING BETTER

𝓝obody was happier about school starting the day after Labor Day than our moms and dads. They were exhausted and as Dad said, "Broke." Their kids had been "running them ragged" and "running wild" all summer. We "ate them out of house and home" and "watched way too much TV on the idiot box."

Our parents, aunts, uncles, and grandparents had run out of fun places to take us like the *Zoo*, the *Admiral, Busch Stadium*, picnics in all of the parks, the *Art Museum* and our beloved *Forest Park Highlands* which had burned down over the summer. During the summer, some St. Ann families went on vacation to places like *Rockaway Beach, Meramec Caverns* and *Silver Dollar City*, or as Dad said, "Steal Your Last Dollar City." The luckier guys went to exotic destinations like *Ruby Falls* and *Lookout Mountain*, Tennessee. The luckiest guys got to swim in the ocean. Every other year, we visited out-of-state relatives to save money on motels.

I've never seen the ocean but we visited the Smoky Mountains on our way to our cousins' house one year.

By the time school started, our parents had run out of chores for us and excuses for why we couldn't do things or go places with our friends. They were sick of us asking to stay up late, camp out in our backyards, stay over at our friends' houses or have our friends stay over at our house. We had wrung our parents out like wet sponges. It was an understatement to say they were ecstatic on our first day of school.

The first day of school meant our parents got order back into their lives, and ours, for the first time in three months. They knew for the next nine months their kids would be in school five days a week except for some scattered holidays and Christmas Vacation. School meant homework and getting to bed early at night. While we were in school, parents only had to deal with us on Friday nights because we got up early Sunday morning for Mass.

On our first day of school, our dads were jealous of our moms. All summer, when our dads left for work, they were doing the happy dance because they didn't have to deal with us all day. When school time came, most of our moms were doing the happy dance because they had the advantage of being home without the kids bugging them.

Most of the nuns and teachers who had to teach us for the next nine months didn't seem all that unhappy. They seemed invigorated by the challenge of making us smart and of course well-behaved. The teachers' summer bliss ended right after the 8:30 a.m. bell rang on the morning of the first day of school. Loudly, the kids walked, in many cases haltingly, into the school's halls and classrooms. The boys wore their brand-new back-to-school clothes. The girls wore freshly pressed school uniforms with knee-high white socks and new shoes. Some of the girls had colorful ribbons or barrettes in their stylish hair to look independent and fashionable. The older girls kept their hair combs and brushes stuffed into their knee-high socks.

On the first day of school, kids had a mixed-bag of feelings that ranged between exhilaration and dire despair. Some, mostly the girls were happy to see the friends they hadn't seen much during the summer. Others, mostly the guys, hated school so much they would've preferred drinking radioactive creek water and eating stinky creek mud than to be in school even with their best friends.

The girls were definitely a lot happier to be back in school than the guys. The girls were almost skipping down the hallways to get to class. The guys' happiness ended on the playground with the sound of the school bell. Then, they took the slow death march into school. We all had to find out who our teacher was and which friends weren't in our class. A lot of my best friends were always in the other class. Did the nuns do that on purpose? Probably. Most of the boys were so nervous they had the collywobbles.

The boys knew the teachers were going to blame us for everything that happened over the next nine months, including snickering, dropped bottles of milk, whispering in class, silent farts, thunderstorms or acts of God. We saw invisible targets on each other's backs. We knew the teachers had predetermined which boy was going to be blamed for codified or imagined school infractions that were accompanied with appropriate penance and pain.

It was a well-known and accepted fact teachers liked girls, even the worst behaved, better than the best-behaved boys.

When something, read that as anything, happened in any room on school property, the teachers' first response was always to blame the nearest boy. Under any atmospheric condition, the teacher scrutinized the boys until they wilted and then she asked, "Which one of you boys did it? I want to give you a chance to come forward." I have seen boys freely admit to doing something even when they didn't do it because of the way a teacher glared at them. Teachers didn't suspect girls misbehaved unless guys weren't in the room. Last year a nun brought a guy into the room just so she could blame him instead of the girls.

When a girl misbehaved, made a noise, mishandled passing a note, whispered too loudly or laughed out loud, they knew instinctively, through a little-researched survival DNA code, to look at the nearest boy. Magically, through genetic code, the guilt felt by the girl automatically transferred to the nearest boy. As her sense of guilt transported to him. Then, his cheeks would turn red and he would start to sweat not because he was at fault but because he knew he was going to be blamed and punished. It's one of the laws of species survival Darwin discussed at length in a treatise that was stolen. The theft was blamed on a man named Edward the Reprehensible (1802-1846). The actual thief was known to be a woman whose name was never divulged.

Today, my heart was filled with despair. I couldn't have worked up a smile even if you handed me a tall glass of cherry-flavored Coca Cola over chipped ice at the Rexall Drug soda counter. I wasn't even happy playing tag before school.

Kickball was my favorite playground sport but nobody thought to bring a ball to school. So, we made do and played tag. Making things worse was some of the girls from our class wanted to flirt with the guys playing tag. This was a first for the guys. We didn't know how to flirt. We showed off instead and acted like the girls were annoying us. Truthfully, we liked their attention.

It was fun showing off until Sister Mary Paul saw the girls and boys teasing each other. Immediately, Sister rushed over and blamed the boys. She threatened the boys with detention if we kept bothering the girls and pointed to the white line painted down the middle of the asphalt playground to separate the girls and the boys' play areas. Naturally, all of the boys' faces turned red, and we began to sweating indicating our guilt even though it was obvious the girls were on our side of the line.

"You boys stay on your side of that white line," Sister commanded, pointing her long index finger at the newly painted white line. "Leave the girls alone."

When she uttered those words, I remembered exactly what I hated most about school. I didn't like bossy nuns and teachers always telling me what to do and watching me like hawks. This year my greatest fear was Sister Mary Regina. Sister Regina was the meanest, bossiest nun at St. Kevin. Our older brothers told us she hated boys more than any of the other teachers hated boys. She didn't even like boys that tucked in their shirts, wrote neatly, completed their homework and earned straight As.

The worst part was that Sister Regina had been teaching fifth-grade forever, and I was going to be in fifth-grade this year. The rumor was Sister wanted and got every boy that hated school the most in her class. Based on those criteria, I knew I was going to be assigned to her class. The only things I liked about school were lunch, recess, art class and school holidays.

After the bell rang, we had to report to the cafeteria to receive our assigned classrooms and teachers. Our names were listed on sheets of paper taped to the wall. The teachers' names were at the top of each page. Slowly, my friends and I trudged over to the two sheets of purple mimeographed paper for fifth-grade students.

I couldn't bring myself to look when Larry said, "Hey, Mickey, we're in the same class this year." That great news still didn't lift my spirits.

"Oh great," I moaned, "We'll be in hell together."

"Who's Miss Kann?" asked Larry.

"I don't know," said Kurt, "But, she's got to be better than Sister Regina. We sure got lucky."

"What? Who?" I asked as I fought my way through the guys to find the sheet with my name. I stood in complete and utter disbelief. I was assigned to Miss Kann's fifth-grade class not Sister Regina's. Who was Miss Kann? Was it a mistake? If it was a mistake would I get caught and be put into Sister Regina's class? I hoped it wasn't a trick to fill me with hope and then flatten me into despair. None of us had ever heard of Miss Kann.

What if Miss Kann was stricter and hated boys even more than Sister Regina? Was it possible the school had gone out and hired a former lion trainer or an ax murderer to get even with us? Maybe that's why my friends and I were put in class together.

"Wait a minute. Where is Stubby Brown? Is he in our class?" I asked. If he was, they were undoubtedly trying to get all of us with one deathblow. It didn't make sense. It had to be a trick.

"Nope," said Jim, "Stubby's in Sister Regina's class." We all laughed at the thought of Stubby's and Sister Regina's wills battling in the same classroom all year. It would be a Battle Royale, and it might've been worth being in her class to watch them tangle every day.

Elated not to be in Sister Regina's class and sad to be back in school, we slowly tramped down the hall to Miss Kann's classroom. We were filled with feelings of dread and gloom not knowing what to expect. John, always the optimist, was the only guy with enough hope to smile.

As we walked into our classroom, we couldn't believe what we saw. We thought our eyes were playing tricks on us. Our fifth-grade teacher, Miss Kann, was the youngest and the prettiest teacher in St. Kevin and possibly the whole world.

Her smile was radiant, her hair was perfect, and she was wearing cute and stylish clothes. My first day of fifth-grade was a daydream instead of the nightmare I had dreamt about all summer.

Wait a minute I thought as I slapped myself in the head to wake up. This had to be a dream. I was asleep and enrolled in Sister Regina's class with Stubby Brown. I must've been caught in an unholy nightmare, but wait, that wasn't right. I knew I was awake. I felt Kurt hitting my arm as he whispered, "Hubba Hubba," smiling and pointing his thumb at Miss Kann. She was the prettiest teacher I had ever seen.

All of the kids were wound up and excited to be in Miss Kann's class. Everyone was going up to her and introducing themselves

before they found a wooden desk to sit down and await instruc-
tions. The seats up front were already taken.

Feeling drugged I realized Larry was dragging me over to meet
Miss Kann. She was standing in front of her desk smiling and
saying hello to everyone. Her smile was so big and so friendly I
was frozen in place. I couldn't move or utter one syllable. Heck,
I couldn't even remember my name or her name or where I was.
I was frozen stiff. Luckily, Larry was holding me up so I didn't
fall. I couldn't mutter a sound. I was bewitched.

Then I heard Larry nervously blather, "Hello, Miss Kann. I'm
Larry, and this is my friend, Mickey McBride. We think you're
beautiful! I mean, we think you're a great teacher. I mean, we're
excited to be in your class because we don't like Sister Regina.
Sister's very mean, and you look so beautiful. I mean nice. May
I clean your chalkboards every day after school, Miss Kann?"

Miss Kann awkwardly smiled as she looked at the two of us.
Then Larry gave Miss Kann his cheesiest smile, and let go of me
so he could step forward and shake her hand. Unwrapped by
Larry's arm, I collapsed backwards to the super glossy and newly
waxed tile floor in a stupor looking up towards Miss Kann. Time
stopped as I lovingly gazed into her horrified eyes. My smile
turned into a grimace when my head splatted on the floor like
a ripe melon. Golden stars and differently colored cartoon birds
circled above my head before I blacked out.

Boys were supposed to be hardy and being called a crybaby was a significant insult. We rarely cried in public. In private, we wailed like babies.

We were taught early in life that inconsequential injuries like knife wounds, chipped teeth, broken legs and arms, falls from trees or bike and getting stitches rarely gave our parents reason to raise an eyebrow until our dads got the medical bills. When medical bills came due, dads preached playground safety and told us to be more careful. Nothing was a better motivator than saving an almighty dollar.

As I slowly gained consciousness and the stars and birds stopped circling overhead, my eyes began to focus, and my mind started to clear. I found myself face-to-face with Miss Kann. I was looking deeply into her beautiful eyes and radiant smile.

I smelled the mint on her breath from her mouthwash. My first thought was, "Am I dead?" My head was resting softly in her lap. I felt cold ice on the back of my head where she was tenderly holding it. There seemed to be a lump the size of a lemon on the back of my head. It was as tender as a broken bone, and I wanted to cry but I didn't want to cry in front of my whole class. I saw my heart beating like a tom-tom through my shirt.

"Are you okay, Mickey?" she asked very softly almost whispering. "Let's call your mom so she can pick you up and take you home."

Groggy, I tried to refocus my eyes which seemed crossed. Slowly, I looked up and around. All of the kids in my class were standing over me looking down. John, Jim and Larry were making kissy lip faces at me. Some of the girls looked worried but most were just annoyed that a guy was getting Miss Kann's attention. Out of the corner of my left eye, or was it my right eye I wasn't sure, I saw Kurt give me the thumbs-up sign. He was pointing to Miss Kann wearing his biggest Cheshire cat smile and slowly shaking his head up and down. He was thinking I set the whole thing up so my head would end up in her lap. Was he crazy?

From the looks on the guys' faces, I was their hero. My thinking processes were beginning to fire, and I started to scheme.

"I feel great, Miss Kann," I lied. "I don't want to miss my first day of class. Do you think I can sit upfront so I can keep an eye on you? I mean, so you can keep an eye on me."

Miss Kann smiled, gave me a wink, and said, "Okay Mickey, let's see how you feel later."

Then, she gently lifted my head off her lap, held on to me tightly, and asked for help to stand me up. John jumped at the chance to be next to her. "I'll help, Miss Kann," as he slyly smiled and pushed the other guys out of our way.

As we slowly stood up, she told the classroom full of kids to take their seats. She, John and I staggered over to the desk right in front of hers. John said, "I better take the one next to Mickey just in case he needs help." Miss Kann nodded agreement. I gave John a wry look as he was getting on my nerves. The other guys jostled and wrestled, forcing the girls out of their way, to get to the other seats around Miss Kann's desk.

It felt like Bizarro world. Everything was backward—like a mirror. Usually, the guys wanted to sit in the back of the classroom. Teachers had to make the guys move to the front so they could blame them for everything. Today, the girls were upset because the boys had pushed them out of their claimed seats in the front.

I felt groggy as I rubbed the lemon-sized knot on the back of my head, but I was sitting in heaven where I could easily watch, Miss Kann. After everyone was settled, we had spelling and math lessons before it was time for lunch.

I was trying to concentrate but it wasn't easy. My head throbbed and the ice was dripping down my back making my shirt wet.

Miss Kann was afraid I had a concussion, and she was probably right. By the end of the morning, all I had written was "Miss Kann can," about 1,000 times in my notebook, which had a photograph of Red Skelton making a funny face on the cover. I really couldn't remember much of what was said. When the lunch bell rang, Miss Kann told me to come back to the classroom after I ate. She didn't want me running and playing outside. She told me I could bring a couple of friends to play some games and that she would stay with us.

You know what happened. Kurt, Jim, Larry, and my new guardian angel, John, followed me like shadows. They acted like they were worried about me. I knew they wanted to hang out with Miss Kann.

As we walked through the classroom doorway, Kurt acted as if he was helping me and said with his fake cheesy smile, "Hi, Miss Kann! We want to spend recess with Mickey. We don't want him to feel lonely," then he gave his sad puppy-dog face.

"That's so sweet of you, Kurt! You, guys, are wonderful friends. What would you like to do during recess?" she asked as she put her lunch things in her drawer.

Perturbed for interrupting my time with Miss Kann I said, "It's okay, Miss Kann. I don't want the guys to miss getting some exercise outside in the fresh air. Beat it, I mean, you guys should go outside and play," I said, sounding pitiful. "I'll be fine here with Miss Kann." I scowled and gently nodded my sore head towards the door.

"No way, Mickey, we want to be here for you," said Jim. He was showing his sweetest and most innocent smile, which cloaked his dastardly intentions of busting in on my time with Miss Kann.

"Then it's decided. What should we do to have some fun?" asked Miss Kann to the group.

Thinking as fast as my muddled mind could process, I said, "Well, I'd like some help doing fractions, Miss Kann. Can you and the guys help me? I didn't understand the lesson today," I said as sincerely as I could without snickering out loud. I hoped my gambit would get rid of the conniving fifth-grade Casanovas who were encroaching on my misfortune.

"We'd be happy to review adding and subtracting fractions with you. They are difficult. Wouldn't we, boys?"

Before she could finish her sentence, Larry and the other Lotharios were running through the doorway. John yelled over his shoulder, "We don't want to get in your way, Miss Kann. If you need to help Mickey with math, we'll go outside to get some exercise. See you later, Mickey."

At last, the guys were gone, and Miss Kann and I were alone. My head was spinning with romantic possibilities. I wanted her to know I was excited to be in her class and in love with her. She was so pretty and such a great teacher.

I couldn't believe my ears when she started talking. "Gosh, Mickey, I'm so excited to be teaching at St. Kevin. We have a great class! Don't we?"

"Yeah, the kids in our class are great, Miss Kann."

"I can't wait to tell my fiancée, Ron, about my first day of teaching. He's going to be so excited for me. He was worried that fifth-grade boys would be troublemakers. If he could just meet you and your friends, he'd think differently. Can you imagine? You guys are great! Except for hitting your head, it's been a fantastic morning. Don't you think, Mickey?"

"Yes, Miss Kann, it's been great," I said sadly as I sat there crestfallen. How did I miss seeing her engagement ring? It must've been the knot on my head. The more she talked the more my head ached. She'd never be my girlfriend. Our romance was over before it started. Who the heck was Ron anyway? He had ruined everything.

"I'm going to tell everybody in our class about my surprise plans for our class after recess. I'll tell you now but you can't tell anybody and spoil the fun, Mickey. Okay? I'm going to let the students use our art class periods to decorate our classroom bulletin boards, and we are going to produce a class play for each holiday. It's going to be a fantastically fun year that everybody's going to remember. I just hope it doesn't go by too fast."

As she spoke, I heard and felt the excitement in her voice. I felt guilty thinking how I had been tricking her all morning. She was so sincere and thoughtful. She really cared about her students. I had never had a teacher like Miss Kann. She was amazing, and it was going to be a spectacular year. As I rubbed the lump on the back of my noggin, I decided to help Miss Kann every way I could.

"Those are great ideas, Miss Kann, and I'm sure excited to be in your class. I'll help any way I can," trying to think my way out of the math problems.

"I'm counting on you, Mickey," she said as she smiled innocently. Let's do some fractions before the other kids come in from recess."

"Sure," I groaned and moaned.

"What's the matter, Mickey?"

"I wonder if we should call Mom, Miss Kann. My head still really hurts. Maybe I should go home and get some rest."

"That's the best idea, Mickey. You've been very brave," she said as she walked me to the principal's office to call Mom. There wasn't any reason to start the school year too quickly. Besides, I needed to rest. My Boy Scout patrol had a meeting after school to plan for the upcoming Jamboree.

❧

MOTHER NATURE'S SON

Everybody admired a man or a woman in a uniform and now that I was a Boy Scout of America my life was like a Norman Rockwell painting. Everybody smiled kindly and nodded knowingly when I walked past in my uniform on my way to a patrol or troop meeting. Most people probably thought I was looking for some good deed to do but usually I was thinking about stuff like baseball, music or girls and not getting caught doing things I wasn't supposed to do. A uniform can hide a lot.

I learned lots of cool stuff in Scouting. I could tie cool rope knots with just a couple of loops that I could use to climb a mountain or tie a boat to a pier or somebody to a tree. Scouting taught us how to set up a tent so the rain didn't run like a river through the middle of it on a stormy night. The older scouts had taught us how to make a cooking fire on a windy day and light a fart with a wooden match. A guy could use two matches but the chances of burning the seat of your pants were a lot higher. They also taught us how to belch loudly by swallowing air.

Scouting was my window to the outside world and our Scoutmaster, Mr. Hunter, opened it wide. Mr. Hunter looked like a Norman Rockwell painting on the cover of the *Saturday Evening Post*. Whenever we had a scouting activity, he was dressed in his clean and pressed uniform with all of his patches neatly sewn on his shirt and his red scout leader woolen jacket. He had uniform shorts for the summer and long pants for the winter. His neckerchief slide, which he had carved, was a bust of Chief Joseph the Chief of the Nez Perce tribe. He wore a flat-brimmed Campaign scouting hat and carried a tall walking staff he carved into a series of rope knots and lashings.

Around our campfires, Mr. Hunter slowly puffed his Meerschaum pipe that was carved into the head of a Bald Eagle. Sitting in his camp chair he puffed his Meerschaum and sent gentle fragrant clouds of cherry smoke towards the stars. Even on the coldest nights he would smile and listen to all of the guys tell ghost stories and have belching contests. He never yelled or got mad. He was happy and content. He seemed to love scouting as much as we loved it. Maybe more.

Neither Mr. Hunter nor Mr. Manhattan, his assistant scoutmaster, ever had to put logs on the troop fire or stir the coals to keep it burning. They taught the oldest scouts to do it, and the older scouts taught the younger scouts, like me, to do it. We fed the fire all day with seasoned wood. At night, we banked it so we'd have coals in the morning to cook. We could start fires using flint, steel and straw or one wooden match. It didn't matter. We were prepared.

Mr. Manhattan was the exact opposite of Mr. Hunter. They were an odd couple and best friends. Mr. Manhattan's uniform was never pressed, and it was missing some patches. He was always telling jokes and playing tricks on the new scouts. Neither he nor Mr. Hunter ever put up our tents, tied our shoes, picked up the campsite or cooked the food. Those jobs were left to the scouts.

I had been excited about the Boy Scout Jamboree at Beaumont for a month. Beaumont was way out in the boonies in "God's country" according to Mr. Manhattan. The Jamboree was a convention of troops from all over our district. Over a thousand scouts were camping out. The troops and patrols competed against each other for honors and awards. When I joined the troop last summer, I was put into a patrol called the Wild Mustangs. Joey was our patrol leader. He made it harder on me than if I was in the Roaring Lions with Johnny as my patrol leader. Joey always gave me more to do than the other guys because I was his younger brother. When I complained he gave me more to do so, I quit complaining.

When we got to Beaumont Friday night, we unpacked the cars and trailers and set up our tents. We worked in the dark. It was hard work lifting and carrying our equipment and getting set up. When we were done and ready for fun, Mr. Manhattan called the new scouts to his tent.

He showed us what looked like a wave at the top of his tent and asked which of us had brought the tent stretcher. No one did and we didn't know what one was. He looked disappointed.

"You're supposed to be prepared guys. You can't depend on your moms out here in the great outdoors," he said slowly shaking his head back and forth, "Tsk, tsk, tsk, boys, new scouts are always supposed to bring the tent stretchers in case of damp nights like tonight. Now, you have to go borrow one from another troop, so we can stretch our tents. Get going." We felt badly we had disappointed Mr. Manhattan and weren't prepared. We'd never even heard of a tent stretcher in Webelos.

We ran off into the dark tramping from one troop site to the next to borrow a tent stretcher. It seemed like all of the new scouts from the other troops had forgotten their tent stretchers too. Every time we'd ask to borrow a stretcher from a scoutmaster, he'd just lent theirs to another troop. So, he'd send us farther down the road to find it. Everybody seemed to be borrowing the only tent stretcher at the Jamboree. We were always 10 minutes behind it and never caught up to it. We were gone for over an hour when we got back to our troop's campsite—empty-handed and tired.

Mr. Manhattan was disappointed but thankfully understanding. As a reward for our effort, after we set up our campsites, he promised to take us snipe hunting. He said the weather conditions were perfect for snipes, and he knew the best place in Beaumont to hunt them. He told us to meet him at the fire with our empty pillowcases in fifteen minutes.

We were more than excited. Mr. Manhattan wasn't letting the older scouts come along, and we were tired of them telling us what to do. It sounded like a great adventure.

None of us had ever seen a snipe. We had only heard about them. We wondered why our Webelos leader had never taught us about tent stretchers or snipes. As we finished setting up, we talked about what snipes looked like and if they were dangerous. The older scouts told us they were small and furry and as fast as a bolt of lightning. We were going to have to be quick to catch them. Fortunately, they told us snipes didn't bite, too hard, and they didn't get rabies. We weren't expected to kill or eat them. It was just fun to catch and release them. The older scouts were disappointed. Anxious, we worked like ants hauling a hamburger to get our chores done to go snipe hunting with Mr. Manhattan.

We had to leave our flashlights and snacks in our tents. Mr. Manhattan said snipes were extremely sensitive to light and their sense of smell was so good they could smell sugar, especially chocolate, from over a mile away. Catching snipes was going to be a wily challenge.

Mr. Manhattan led the way up the woody hillside. We trailed behind him full of excitement and just a little foreboding. At the beginning of our trek, our steps were light and quick but as we trudged further and as the hills got steeper Mr. Manhattan had to urge us forward with whispers of encouragement and hints about the best way to hold our pillowcases.

Every five minutes or so we'd stop to practice the best stances for trapping a snipe. He was a master snipe trapper. He knew everything about them. He regaled us with thrilling tales about courageous scouts who trapped gigantic snipes that looked as sweet as a bunny rabbit but were as fast as the head of a cobra.

He knew everything about snipes and he answered every question we had about what they ate, how they birthed their young and most importantly how they thought and acted.

He felt good about tonight because there was a new moon and so little light in the sky. We could barely see each other without our flashlights. The snipe's major weakness was eyesight. They didn't see well but they had a better sense of smell than a hound dog, and they heard better than a bat. Another weakness was snipes emitted a shrill whistle when they hunted for food. He expected one of us was going to trap a record-breaking snipe tonight and I intended that record-breaking snipe hunter to be me. As I tramped along, I practiced quickly swooping the ground with my pillowcase. I was prepared.

As we hiked for what seemed like a few miles, Mr. Manhattan started dropping us off one-by-one on the tree-covered hillside. Each Scout was armed only with his pillowcase.

As each Scout marched off to his assigned outpost, Mr. Manhattan would put his finger to his lips and whisper, "Stay brave and keep your pillowcase at the ready, scout. Be patient. Listen for the low whistle of the snipe." Then he'd pat the guy on his shoulder and the rest of us would steal away quietly.

Mr. Manhattan was a diabolical mastermind of cunning and daring. He was probably one of the most skilled snipe hunters in the world. We were blessed to have him as our teacher.

Snipes were speedy and had a nervous temperament. His ingenious plan was to place us along the hillside like a string of Christmas lights. Then he was going to herd the snipes in our direction by beating the ground with a stick. As he beat the ground like a drum, he was going to imitate a wild turkey's hunting call. The only natural predator quick and wily enough to catch a snipe was the wild turkey. Go figure.

I stood attentively at my post and recounted every sage lesson from his whispered homilies up the hillside. I held my pillowcase lightly in both hands with my arms outstretched just the way he had showed us. I planned to snatch every snipe that dared dart in my direction.

Trying to figure out how to snatch more than one snipe, it dawned on me I hadn't heard a whistle or seen a wisp of anything or anyone for over an hour. Feeling drowsy, I hoped the guys hadn't forgotten me after they caught dozens of snipes and walked back to camp. I was worried they had scared the snipes from my part of the hillside as they trudged away.

Disappointed by my bust of a hunt, I worked my way back to the troop's campsite. It was dark and late. More than once I thought I heard a snipe's whistle, a bear or even a werewolf. I figured Frankenstein wasn't this far out in the boonies.

When I made it back to camp, there was Mr. Hunter and Mr. Manhattan sitting around the campfire. One was laughing and the other was smiling with a fragrant cloud over his head. As I plodded up to the fire, Mr. Manhattan sang out, "How many did you catch, Mickey? Any record breakers?" He was eating a Hershey candy bar.

"None," I said dejectedly. "I did everything just the way you told me. I don't know what I did wrong. How about the other guys? Did they get any record breakers?"

"Not a one," he said, shaking his head back and forth, "And the darnedest thing happened."

"What," I asked.

"Remember how I told you snipes are wily? Well, those crafty critters came into camp after we left. They pilfered a lot of the guy's treats especially the chocolate. You better check your booty."

"Oh no," I screamed over my shoulder as I ran towards my tent, "thanks for taking us snipe hunting, Mr. Manhattan. It was fun, good night!"

I slept like a rock after running around all night. It was near impossible to wake up early on a chilly morning to build the patrol's cooking fire. Luckily, the snipes didn't filch all of my Oreos so I grabbed one and popped it into my mouth. The patrols had to get ready for their cooking tests. Cooking was the first of 10 tests each patrol had to take. The patrols with the highest scores at the end of the day won honor ribbons, and the troops with the most honor patrols won troop honor ribbons. Boy Scout Troop 643 was one of the most decorated troops in the St. Louis Area Council.

Dave and I were firemen. We had to build our patrol's campfire from the coals still glowing from the night before. We had to gather enough kindling and firewood to last all day including three meals. It took a mountain of wood. The guys relished a roaring fire especially when it was cold outside. Roaring fires were mesmerizing. Everyone sat transfixed watching the flare-ups, and listening to the pops, crackles, and hisses. After the fire was sizzling, the older guys would finally climb out of their almost warm sleeping bags.

A scoutmaster from another troop named Mr. Dale came to our patrol's campsite to judge the breakfast we were cooking. Judges graded patrols on how good the food tasted and cleanliness of our camp kitchen. The older guys didn't want to take a chance by having the younger guys cook. There was too much at stake.

Mr. Dale asked to see our breakfast menu while he inspected our camp kitchen which was a large wooden box on wooden legs. It was stuffed with packaged food, pots, pans and silverware. He was surprised when Donny handed him a steaming cup of 'Cowboy Coffee.'

"Well, I've never been given a cup of real coffee before, boys. Patrols usually give me a cup of instant coffee. It smells strong, thanks! How'd you make it?"

"Thank you, sir. We made it just the way my Grandpa said to make it," winked Donny. Dave and I smiled at each other knowing we had just scored some brownie points with Mr. Dale for the coffee.

Donny led the visiting scoutmaster through our camp kitchen showing him that all of our dishes were clean and that there weren't any webs or bugs lurking.

While Donny played tour guide, Joey, Greg and Billy were working over the open fire cooking breakfast. Dave and I kept busy feeding small pieces of firewood into the fire to keep the temperature up and pouring water on the few renegade flames that inevitably flared up.

Who doesn't love the smell and sound of sizzling bacon especially when it's cooked over an open fire? Billy had fried strips of bacon woven into four-piece squares in our giant cast-iron skillet. The bacon grease was popping as Greg cracked the large eggs onto the bacon weaves in the skillet. We called them "Eggs in a Nest." Bacon and eggs fried in an iron skillet were relatively easy to cook even on an open fire. The real challenge this morning that would make or break our grade was pancakes.

Cooking pancakes over an open fire in an iron skillet was tricky. You had to grease your pan in butter or vegetable oil to fry them. Grease made pancakes burn and char. Most pancakes that Boy Scouts fried were rubbery and burnt. They made better Frisbees than pancakes. To eat them, you needed a sharp knife a good set of choppers and a stomach like a garbage disposal. We were taking a big chance putting pancakes on our menu. Most patrols didn't make pancakes because they were too risky. We didn't have Crisco Cooking Oil but we did have Joey.

Joey spent his summer researching the best modern ways to cook over an open fire. Boys eat just about anything. We cooked breakfast, lunch and dinner, including Spam, worms and crickets in our cast-iron skillet. We could we could cook everything in our skillet, and it was iron. In other words, our cast iron skillet was indestructible.

If you hand a boy a brand-new rubber ball he will see if he can throw it so hard it splits in half when it hits the wall. Or, he will bounce it so hard on the ground it will penetrate the Ozone. After a half an hour, that brand-new ball will be destroyed; smashed to smithereens or look so old the family dog won't play with it.

If you give a boy a sturdy stick as a hiking staff, he will use it as a bat and smack everything within reach to see how strong it and he are.

If you give a boy a cast iron skillet, well, you get the idea. Boys used cast iron skillets to swat just about anything including baseballs, flies and friends. Iron skillets didn't make good Frisbees but we could cook a meal or drive a tent peg with our cast iron skillet and we did.

It was Joey's job to cook the pancakes for the Jamboree. We planned to serve Cowboy Coffee, Eggs in the Nest and steaming hot pancakes to Mr. Dale. Joey even had Dave and I warm the Karo syrup with a stern warning not to boil it. He took control of the fire and strategically placed the grill at the exact height he wanted for the pancakes. Then as we all watched Joey asked Greg to move the frypan with the Nests to the cooler side of the fire.

Ceremoniously, Joey carefully pulled something wrapped in a dishtowel out of his knapsack. Billy sprinkled cinnamon over the thick Betty Crocker Bisquick Pancake Mix batter as he brought it over to the fire. Smoothly, Joey placed what looked like a sizeable tan plate with shiny silver metal handle on the grill and ladled three large pancakes onto it. Then, he unwrapped a wide plastic spatula from another dishtowel. As soon as the bubbles popped on top of the pancakes, Joey flipped them with his special spatula.

We all gasped and Mr. Dale exclaimed, "Well, I'll be darn boys! Those are the most scrumptious looking pancakes I've ever seen and hope to eat. My own wife's pancakes don't look golden brown. Yours aren't burned. What kind of a pan is that? I've never even seen one before," he said as he sipped his steaming cup of coffee.

After he put his coffee down, Mr. Dale slathered real butter and poured warm amber-colored syrup over the yummiest stack of pancakes any of us had ever seen. I used the moment of bon-homie to swoop-in for my stack of honey-colored hotcakes and then I moved to the sidelines to eat and listen.

"Well, Mr. Dale I'm not sure the Mustangs should give away our secret," Joey kidded.

"I understand Joey, but I have to know so I can tell my wife how to make them," he chuckled, "Please tell me. These pancakes are as delicious as they are good-looking. By the way boys, nice touch with the warm syrup!"

"Over the summer, I discovered a frying pan coated with Teflon that can be used on an open fire. Food doesn't stick to Teflon. We didn't have to use oil to fry our pancakes. Since we didn't use oil the pancakes didn't burn," smiled Joey. "Please don't tell anybody but your wife, Mr. Dale. If you do, every patrol will have one next year."

"I won't tell anybody," said Mr. Dale as he wrote down a score of 100 points out of 100 points. None of us stopped smiling as we washed the dirty dishes and hid our Teflon pan and plastic spatula.

For lunch, we fried bologna in the cast iron skillet because we liked our bologna a little burned for our sandwiches. After our Semaphore signaling and first aid challenges, the guys were getting worried about our orienteering challenge. It was usually one of the hardest competitions of the Jamboree.

The guys were nervous because I had forgotten to wear my Keds. The older Mustangs told me to measure and mark my Keds by inches on their sides and their bottoms. They planned to have rulers on my feet so we could make exact measurements during our orienteering challenge. So far, we had only lost 20 total points out of a possible 800 points. We were scorching the challenges, and it looked like we might set a troop record. The guys didn't want to be off an inch in orienteering, so I needed my marked-up Keds. I marked my Keds with a black ballpoint pen around the sides and on the bottom of each shoe.

I was running back from our campsite as fast as I could when I came across a kid named Pat sitting on a log spitting into a creek. He was from another troop and was just hanging out.

We liked each other immediately so I challenged Pat to a spitting contest. It was cool to watch how fast our spit hit the creek from the large rock we were standing on and float away. He beat me by spitting farther down the creek than me and showed me it was essential to arch and snap my neck at just the right moment to get my spit as far as possible. I promised myself to practice more in the future.

Next, Pat challenged me to a jumping contest. "Sure," I said, feeling good at learning a new life skill but forgetting about the orienteering challenge. "What're you thinking?"

"Well, can you jump across the creek? I can," crowed Pat. "Let's see who can jump the farthest across the creek. The guy that jumps the farthest wins," declared Pat. "I'll go first."

We jumped down from the rock and walked over to the edge of the creek. We were uneasily rubbing our chins while we searched for the best takeoff and landing spots. It had rained earlier in the week so the stream was muddier, deeper and broader than usual. I figured we had to jump at least 15 feet to clear the creek. We were worried. We wished we had thought of a different dare but boys will be boys.

Without stalling, Pat made his decision on his path and backed off from the creek. He ran as long and fast as he could manage while dodging the trees and fallen logs. Pat decided on a spot higher than the rest of the bank for his leap. He was running fast as he hit his spot and launched himself like a rocket.

I thought Pat was going to clear the creek until he dropped like a rock into the deepest part of the creek. The current was so fast he went under and came up drenched. He was spitting muddy water when he yelled, "Is this where I landed? I'll stand here until you jump to mark my spot."

After seeing Pat's failed leap, I lost confidence in my launch strategy. I decided to move my spot further up the creek in hopes of a higher takeoff. Hopefully, added height would carry me across the creek. As I surveyed the swishing muddy water, I remembered that the guys were waiting for me and my marked shoes. How had I forgotten the guys?

Motivated, I knew I had to clear the creek and get to the guys as quickly as I could. On the outside chance it might work, I tried to de-materialize and re-materialize on the other side of the creek. Dang. It didn't work.

Another idea occurred to me. Wouldn't it be cool if I flew to the guys? They would be blown away if they saw me soaring through the sky and land right in the middle of the Mustangs like Superman. It'd be so cool. I had always wanted to be able to fly. Heck, I even dreamed about flying.

The dreams I liked best were my dreams about flying. Everyone dreamed about being able to soar in the blue sky higher than a kite among the white puffy clouds. Whether you were flying as a supersonic McDonnell Douglas jet, a fire-breathing dragon or a lowly sparrow on wing, being able to fly would be very cool.

I had to force myself to quit daydreaming because I needed to jump across the creek and find the guys. I couldn't de-materialize or fly, so I had to jump. I felt confident as I visualized my jump and backed off to get a running start for my launch.

I ducked under and stepped over some saplings to get to my starting point. Sighing and taking a deep breath, I sprinted through the underbrush until I hit my takeoff point. I closed my eyes and strained to leap as far and as high as I could. The sensation of the crisp fall wind slapping my face revitalized me and gave me the feeling of being a bird in flight. Momentarily, I felt like an eagle and briefly flapped my arms to gain altitude.

When I opened my eyes, I realized I wasn't going to get even close to landing on the other side. I prepared for a crash and splash landing in the cold muddy creek. Thankfully, the water broke my fall as I dropped into the icy cold creek. I was drenched and my teeth were chattering.

I couldn't budge my feet as I tried to walk out of the creek. My feet were stuck up to my ankles in the muddy creek bottom. It felt like I was sinking deeper. I grunted to pull one leg at a time free from the sticky gummy muck. My feet barely wiggled must less budged, and I was getting worried. Anxiously, I looked up to see Pat standing on the shore. He was extending a long limb out to me. He was shivering, when he said, "Grab the stick, Mickey. I'll pull you out."

I grabbed the stick. Pat pulled and I held on tightly. My right foot pulled free from the gelatinous muck that had me tacked to the creek bottom. Momentarily relieved, I realized that the muck had sucked my Ked and my sock cleanly off my foot.

"I lost my shoe. Stop pulling Pat," I yelled as I ducked my head under the water and felt around creek's leafy muddy bottom for my shoe. It was nowhere to be found. What was I going to do? At least I still had one shoe for orienteering. With my head above water, Pat pulled the stick again. I was afraid to put my right foot on the creek bottom in case it got stuck again. Then, with a sucking sensation, my left foot suddenly shot free, and Pat pulled me to shore. I had lost both Keds and both socks. I was shivering and dejected as I slithered onto the muddy bank soaked and shoeless. I lost my shoes and the jumping contest.

Pat, shivering from being cold and wet, was laughing so hard he was crying. We were covered in mud. I was laughing because that's what our predicament deserved. I was crying because I knew the Mustangs were already mad at me and losing my shoes made things worse. No matter what I did from this moment everyone was going to be mad at me and blame me for whatever happened. I couldn't win.

Slipping and sliding in my bare feet to stand on the slick muddy creek bank, I wiped the mud from my eyes. "Let's make a fire and dry off, Mickey."

"I wish I could but I have to find my patrol, Pat. They're going to be worried," I said as I waved and trotted off along the path and stepped on a rock. "Ouch! You won Pat," I yelled over my shoulder. "Nice jump!"

Thanks, Mickey, nice meeting you!" he yelled back. Sadly, Pat and I never saw each other again.

My trot through Beaumont to find the Mustangs gave me a chance to think through my dilemma and decide what I was going to tell the guys. I didn't want them to be mad because I forgot my shoes and then for losing them goofing off with Pat.

During my reflective trot, I decided it would be best if we put this unfortunate incident behind us as quickly as possible. We needed to focus on becoming a first-time Honor Patrol. I rationalized, philosophically speaking, that the events of the day couldn't be changed. It was up to me to help the guys forget what had happened.

My marked Keds were gone forever. Nothing could bring them back. Was it okay for me to lie about what happened for the good of the patrol? If I didn't full-out lie, could I adjust the facts a little?

We started every Boy Scout meeting by standing with our patrol in a single-file line looking at the American and our troop's flags. While giving the three-finger salute, as a troop, we proudly recited the Scout Oath and the Scout Law after we said the Pledge of Allegiance. First, we said our Oath.

"On my honor, I will do my best to do my duty to God and my country and to obey the Scout Law; To help other people at all times; To keep myself physically strong, mentally awake, and morally straight."

Then, we said the Scout Law.

"A Scout is trustworthy, loyal, helpful, friendly, courteous, kind, obedient, cheerful, thrifty, brave, clean, and reverent."

In deep soulful reflection as I ran, I recited those two all-encompassing Boy Scout guidelines. Faster than a speeding bullet my lawyer-like 24 jewel Timex brain locked onto important facts.

Neither the Oath nor the Law directly said a Scout can't omit or colorfully exaggerate a fact here or there. Neither said anything about being truthful. They didn't say a Scout couldn't enhance truth if circumstances warranted an adjustment of the facts for the greater good or to do a good deed.

For example, let's say a young boy was told by his mom to wait for her in a cave. Let's assume he, and I suppose her, didn't know a man-eating bear was in the cave. Further, the boy won't let you rescue him because his mom told him not to leave the cave. Is it okay to tell a lie to get him out of the cave? Eureka! It was okay to recalibrate the facts if your intentions were honorable. Briefly, I thought about becoming a lawyer someday.

Losing my shoes in the muddy creek was beginning to feel like a religious experience. I'm not talking on the level of a Lourdes miracle or sainthood but possibly a reduction in the number of days I would spend in Purgatory. As I thought about religion, my conscience split into two personalities, one on each shoulder.

As my altar boy conscience debated with my Boy Scout conscience, I determined the Mustangs might have inadvertently and unintentionally cheated if I hadn't lost my shoes. Was this Divine Intervention? Was God working a miracle, however minor, through me? Did He cause me to fall into the creek and lose my Keds?

Upon deeper reflection I decided God, through me, might've saved us from a venial sin but probably not a mortal sin.

Shivering yet sanguine with my newly found spiritual enlightenment, I found the Mustangs on a hillside deep into Camp Beaumont. My clothes were frozen stiff. They looked like they were made out of frozen mud. They cracked more than bent. My feet were red, frozen and numb. The guys were sitting around a small fire scowling like a bunch of nuns. I shuffled up to the warm fire and with some difficulty sat down to thaw out.

"Where have you been, Mickey?" demanded Joey as the guys gawped and chortled and threw a litany of questions at me. It felt like I was in Confession.

"What happened, Mickey? You look like a statue."

"Where are your shoes and socks? Have you gone wacky running around in your bare feet?"

"We've been waiting a long time. We trusted you, Mickey. You let us down."

Just as I was about to explain the situation and instill confidence in the patrol, Joey coldly said, "Go back to the campsite and get cleaned up, Mickey. We're going without you to the rest of the challenges. Have the fire ready for dinner when we get back."

Then Joey stood up and led the guys to the orienteering challenge leaving me behind. None of the guys looked back at me not even Joey.

As I sat alone feeling sorry for myself and warming my feet and hands, I realized nobody, not even Joey, asked me if I was okay.

Staring into the fire, I decided to find some new best friends that cared about me. Joey was acting like a darn adult bossing me around and telling me what to do all of the time. I even started thinking about quitting the Mustangs or maybe even the Boy Scouts altogether. I put out the small fire and trotted back to the campsite careful to avoid the muddy creek.

I decided right then and there, I wasn't going trick or treating with Joey this year. He wasn't my best friend anymore.

&

CHAPTER 4

WORKING CLASS HERO

I felt like our neighbor's dog, Mooch. He'd stick his head out the side window of their Ford station wagon to feel the wind in his face. I was coasting so fast down the hill with the wind in my face that the fresh fall air brought tears to my eyes. I was on my new metallic blue Schwinn Racer that I had gotten for my birthday. What's as cool as free birthday stuff? Nothing, except the granddaddy of them all, free presents for Christmas.

I had wanted a new bike for the last two years. Today, I was pretending my bike was a motorcycle like Streak's. I used clothes-pins to clip some of my old baseball "flip cards" onto the fender so they "flicked" across the spokes as I sped down the hill. I was riding to pick up Mom in another area of St. Ann off Cypress Road. The kids in that part of the city went to St. Mary's Catholic School or St. Ann public school and Pattonville High School.

Dad was miffed. Mom had made a decision without talking to him about it. She just made up her mind and did it. Joey didn't think anything about it but I was a little nervous. Mom was very sure of her decision. She wasn't about to change her mind for anyone not even Dad, and he asked her to change it a lot. She was definite. There wasn't anything anyone could say or do to change her mind.

I always knew I could count on Mom whether I needed her help or not. When I was younger, she did everything for me. She took me to the library, read to me and crawled on the floor to play with me. Every night she tucked me into bed with a hug and a kiss. Mom was a lot of fun, and I always knew she was home waiting for me.

She did all of the grocery shopping and was there to fix all of our breakfasts, lunches and dinners. Every summer she took Joey and me on field trips to different parks around St. Louis, the Zoo and the SS Admiral. She even made sure we went to the Art Museum and the St. Louis Symphony once a year even though I didn't want to go. She took me to the doctor when I got hurt and picked me up from school when I got sick.

Mom went to all of our baseball games and cheered louder than anyone. She'd even tell the umpire, nicely, if she thought he'd made a bad call.

Mom had two rules in life for me. I had to wear clean underwear in case something happened and I had to go to the doctor's office. And, I had to keep a dime in my pocket in case I had to use a phone to call home. Mom was my best friend and my best fan.

One time, a bunch of scalawags trapped us and held us prisoner at knifepoint in their fort. Mom found us and chased those bullies to their home to tell their parents. She even called the police. We never wondered where Mom was because Mom was always where you needed her to be. Home.

Mom was our secretary. She always made sure we did our homework and studied for our tests. She always knew where and when we had to be to do something. Whether it was a Boy Scout's meeting, a camping trip, a baseball game or a practice. Mom always made sure we had something to eat, and that we left early enough to be on time. She was never late.

It wasn't easy to do things that we weren't supposed to do because Mom was always around at just the wrong time. She was like the gypsy mind reader at the Royal American Carnival who wore a brightly colored scarf and big hoop earrings. It was uncanny. She always knew I wasn't telling the whole truth and nothing but the truth about where I had been or what I had been doing.

She said things like, "Don't you make a face at me, Mickey McBride, or I'll ground you for a week," when she had her back towards me and was fixing dinner. How did she know I was making a face? Or she said, "Tell me where you and your friends are really going or I'll ground you for a week. Don't dare lie to me. You know, I'll know you're lying to me."

Mom said she got premonitions about Joey and me because she had a mother's intuition whatever that meant. All I knew was whenever I had some neat idea about doing something that I wasn't supposed to do, like when we rode our bikes to the Missouri River, I tried not to think about it around her. I could never tell when she was reading my mind.

Mom and Dad usually agreed on things but not always. I remember in 1960 they disagreed about the presidential election. Mom voted for John Kennedy, and Dad voted for Richard Nixon. He was upset for months afterward and blamed Mom for anything that went wrong in the world. She didn't care. I remember him saying, "All you did was cancel my vote." She responded, "Well, all you did was cancel my vote," and then they both walked to different corners of the house until they were happy again.

This was the same way. They disagreed, and I didn't see how that would change.

I wasn't really sure how to feel about Mom's decision to become an Avon lady. I didn't know whether to be angry like Dad or not care like Joey. I liked knowing Mom was home and that I could find her when I needed her. Then again, it might've made my life easier if Mom was busy and not home using her mother's intuition.

Mom decided to become an Avon lady after her discussion with Sister Lois about Joey going to high school. Sister wanted Joey to go to a private Catholic high school. Dad said it would be too expensive to go to private high school. He wanted Joey and me to go to a public high school like he and Mom did. Mom decided to get a job as an Avon lady to pay Joey's tuition for a private high school.

Most of my friends' moms didn't work out of their homes. Mom was a rebel defying what my Dad wanted her to do. He wanted her to be home. She wanted to earn money and be independent.

To allay Dad's concerns, Mom told him she'd always be home when we were home from school. During the summer, she said Joey was old enough to watch me. He wasn't convinced but she took the job anyway.

It was Saturday and I was riding my bike to meet Mom at a house in her Avon territory. Dad had our car so I had to pick up Mom and give her a ride home on the crossbar of my Schwinn. When I got to St. Regina Lane, I met a couple of brothers named Ed and Henry. They invited me to go play in the creek, and I was wavering when Mom walked out of a house. She was saying goodbye to a mother with a little girl hanging on her leg. It was their house so I promised them I'd be back someday to play.

Mom slung her large Avon bag over my handlebars and said, "Take me home slowly through the park, Driver."

She laughed, and I puffed all the way home. It wasn't easy peddling up the long St. Stephen hill even on my new Schwinn Racer. It was a lot easier on me though than her butt sitting on the crossbar of my bike. She never complained. She talked all the way home about whether I had done my chores and my homework.

"Can I go with Dutch to the garden today after lunch? He needs help to pick the pumpkins and close the garden for winter."

"Don't you want to hang out with Joey and your friends, Mickey?" she asked. "You don't need to work today. It's so pretty outside."

Mom knew Joey and I weren't hanging out together anymore and that we were acting cool to each other around the house. We stopped joking and horsing around ever since the Boy Scout Jamboree when Joey got mad about nothing.

I didn't care. Joey acted like a jerk, and I wasn't going to apologize. I had a lot of friends. I didn't need to hang out with him. Besides, Joey couldn't do anything anyway. He was caddying at Westwood Country Club with his friends.

Some of the older guys had started caddying at Westwood. They were paid six bucks to carry two large bags of golf clubs for 18 holes. It was hard work but it was cool hanging out in the caddy shack without parents telling them what to do.

When Joey caddied, he hitchhiked to Westwood. He would get there before seven in the morning. If he got an early loop, he could get a second loop after lunch. Joey made twelve bucks a day if he carried two golf bags for 36 holes. It was a king's ransom, and he was home by dinner but he was exhausted.

Phil's brother told him caddies sat around the caddy shack and played poker, smoked cigarettes, drank soda, talked trash and cussed at each other between loops or when it rained. He said rookie caddies got nicknames, like 'Useless,' 'Beans,' and 'Fart-head.' The older caddies constantly harassed rookies, and rookies got the worst golfers for loops. The best part was shuttling golf carts around the course. It sounded like a lot of fun. I wanted to caddy but I was too young.

"Heck Mom, Dutch is my pal. I've been working in the garden since I was a little kid. Besides, I need to bring back some pumpkins to sell for Halloween."

Dutch lived across the street. He didn't have a son. He had teenage daughters that drove him crazy because all they talked about was boys. Even his little tan Chihuahua was a girl but he named her Jaws.

Dutch was the biggest man on our street, and he had the loudest laugh. He was a train engineer who worked the overnight shift. Before I was old enough to go to school, I hung out with him because Joey and the older guys were at school.

Dutch had a faded red 1948 Ford pickup truck that we drove to the farm. He hand-painted a sign on the truck's doors that said, "Dutch's Prickly Porcupine Farm" in white letters. Everybody would stop him and ask him about porcupine farming. He'd laugh while he told them whopper stories always looking mock-serious. He loved to sigh and tell them how difficult it was to hold baby porcupines to hand feed them, and how many times he got stuck milking mother porcupines. People believed every word Dutch said. Afterward, they would walk away in awe shaking their heads from side to side. We would just look at each other and laugh. Each time he'd tell the story, it would get longer, funnier and more detailed.

Riding in his truck was the best part of going to Dutch's garden. He'd let me ride in the back of his pickup on the wooden bed all of the way down the St. Charles Rock Road to the Missouri Bottom Road. That's how I learned where the Missouri River was. All of my friends were jealous. Occasionally, I'd take one of them with us so they could ride in the back of the truck with me.

Today, I was taking Dave to the garden with us. He was excited to go and he was a good worker.

The "Garden of Eating," as Dutch dubbed it, was almost two acres. We grew white and yellow corn, tomatoes, cucumbers, peppers, potatoes, radishes, carrots, cabbage, green beans, apples, peaches, pumpkins, and my personal favorite watermelons. By this time of year, everything had been picked and eaten except pumpkins, and that was good news for me.

We took most of the food we grew home to eat. Anything our families didn't eat, Dutch would let me sell around the neighborhood. He never wanted any of the money. He said he just liked my company.

We had a tradition. The first thing I did when we got to the garden was find a perfectly ripe watermelon. It was my job to carry it over to a sharp rock and smash it wide open. Then we picked up the pieces and ate them the rest of the time we were working in the garden. We saved the seeds to plant the following year.

When we arrived, I let Dave smash our last watermelon of the season. It was always fun to watch. We would've never been allowed to do something crazy like purposefully smash a watermelon. Our parents would've grounded us, and we would've been picking up seeds for a week. Not Dutch, he didn't even care when we spit seeds at each other. Our parents would've screamed like banshees. It was always fun to be with Dutch.

The first time Dave shyly dropped the watermelon down on the rock. It barely cracked open. He was embarrassed until Dutch said, "Smash that sucker, Dave."

With a big smile, Dave picked it up over his head and slammed it down like Dick the Bruiser putting a body slam on Cowboy Bob Ellis on Channel 11's Wrestling at the Chase. It split wide open. The last watermelon of the season always tasted the best; it was exceptionally bright red, sweet and juicy. I'm not sure why.

After we ate the melon and spit some seeds at each other, we got to work. We fed our autumn bonfire with the brown stalks and vines we gathered in the garden and dragged to the pile.

There were some random vegetables and fruit still hanging around that we plucked and put in wooden bushel baskets. Afterwards, Dave and I gathered all of the pumpkins and put them into a pile by the pickup truck. It was hard work.

The pumpkins were a big plus to me. Dutch let me sell the extra ones our families didn't carve for Halloween or cook down for pumpkin pie at Thanksgiving.

Selling the extra vegetables and fruit to our neighbors from my wagon added up to a tidy sum. Whenever I took Dutch his half, he'd say, "Go buy yourself something you want but can't afford with my part, Mickey." I bought a pocketknife last summer. Like I said, Dutch was my pal, my best friend.

After a couple of hours, Dutch told us to take a break. He suggested I take Dave to see the Missouri River while he pulled the rest of the plants and fed them into the smoky fire.

We were happy for the break as we kicked dirt at each other and jogged to the river. It was about three-quarters of a mile beyond a line of big Sycamore trees standing guard. If Dave and I knew anything we knew how to explore and have fun.

Once we got to the river, we started slinging the biggest rocks we could pick up along the bank into the brown foam to see who made the biggest splash. The biggest rocks took both of us to pick up and heave-ho. They sounded like bodies hitting the water; there was an enormous plop before the splash. We also picked up small flat stones we skipped over the top of the water. The most times we were able to skip them was seven times. We strolled along the bank until we felt bored and headed back to the garden. Dutch was probably wondering where we were.

As we threw dust bombs at each other, and walked across weedy river bottom fields, we blundered upon the most ginor-mous pumpkins, or just about anything else, either of us had ever seen. Together, we couldn't have lifted one off of the ground. They were humongous.

There were about a dozen basking in the field. They were a deep, bright orange and most were heavily tinted in various shades of green and white up their sides. A few were reddish. Weirdly, they had a human quality to them. Each looked utterly different, yet the same, from the other. A few had deep wrinkly skin with thick gnarled stems. Others had baby smooth skin. The pumpkins were different sizes and shapes, and they had bumps and lumps that looked variously like ears, noses and eyes. Each reminded me of a Mother Goose drawing of Humpty Dumpty. They looked like colossal orange heads lying in the field.

Each was tethered to the patch with a knobby vine as thick as my arm with dark green leaves as big as my face. All were taller than Dave and most were taller than me. They weighed four or five times more than we did, together. They were mammoth, and their eerie appearance left us feeling uneasy. We had never seen anything like them.

The orange pumpkins that we grew in the garden were about the size of a basketball and easy to lift and carry. The biggest ones were maybe 15 pounds. I hauled several at a time in my rusty, red wagon to sell to neighbors.

Just as I grabbed one of the gnarly vines to scramble up the side of the largest pumpkin a shotgun blast pierced the cold air. The explosion scared the bejeebers out of us as thousands of blackbirds launched from the pumpkin patch and nearby trees into the air. They instantly went flapping and screeching into the beautiful fall sky. It looked like a scary scene from the movie, "The Birds" that I had seen at the Airway Drive-In over the summer.

The blast sounded so close Dave and I dropped face-first onto the ground. We covered our heads with our hands as we spit dust out of our mouths. We laid quietly spitting and shaking, when we heard a gruff growly voice command, "Stand up, you pumpkin smashing varmints and look me straight in the eye!"

As we shakily stood up, we saw an old man pointing a double-barreled shotgun at us. He looked like a grizzled scarecrow dressed in patched raggedy farmer's clothes with a beat-up black felt hat. His droopy hat covered his long, dirty, straw-like gray hair sticking out from under the black brim. His hair matched his long dirty gray beard which held small bits of what looked like his breakfast and maybe lunch too. He was so filthy he looked like he had been rolling in the dust with us. His eyes pierced my soul. I felt ice-cold like I was dead or floating in a cold river. My knees were knocking.

"We didn't smash any of your pumpkins, Mister," I stammered.

"This is the first time we've seen them," pleaded Dave. Our heads nodded and our knees knocked in agreement.

"Don't lie to me, you sneaky little cockroaches," he snarled, moving his shotgun to cradle it in the crook of his left arm. "I ought to shoot you right now for thinking about smashing one of my boys. They're family," he sniffed and wiped his nose on his dirty coat sleeve, "Do you know how much love and attention it takes to grow a pumpkin that big from a seed you little weasels?"

"No, sir," we cried out covering our heads. We wished we had never seen his creepy pumpkins.

"What's going on, Poppa?" screeched what sounded like a woman. We couldn't see her clearly because she was blocking the sun, which was low in the sky. "Are these the killers that smashed our Jack into smithereens?"

"I think so, Momma," he said, giving us the evil eye. He was so close I smelled the food in his beard.

"No, we didn't Mister, honest," I said, making the Scout sign. "We didn't smash Jack. We don't live here. We just came out here today to help Dutch with his garden. That's all. Honest."

"Dutch? Well, why ain't you over at his place instead of over here smashing our boys?"

"We haven't seen any of your boys, sir. We don't know them, and we wouldn't hurt them if we did. We just saw these giant pumpkins. That's all. We've never seen pumpkins this big before. Have we, Dave?"

"Nope," gulped Dave, "never."

"These pumpkins are our boys you slithering snakes," screeched the old lady. As she stepped out from behind the man. She was dressed like an evil witch. She had a dark brown cloak draped over her long black dress matching the color of her pointy wide-brimmed bonnet. She had a looped thick leather belt clutched in a death grip on her right hand. She was swaying it back and forth as she gave us her evil eye up and down very slowly. Her gnarled claw of a hand was rubbing her hairy chin which had a big mole with hair growing out of it. Her mole looked like a miniature pumpkin. It was hard not to stare.

"What should we do with you two pumpkin pillagers? We saw you getting ready to smash Freddie just now. Should we cook you up and eat you? Should we lock you up in a pumpkin? Better yet I'm going to give your backsides a whipping until they're bright red. Hold them, Poppa," she screeched as she stepped forward. "I'm going to whip each of them with 10 smacks right on their butts. They aren't going to hurt our boys again," she squawked.

"No Ma'am, please, we're sorry. We didn't mean to hurt Freddie," we sang in chorus as we flopped down on the dusty ground to cover our butts. I thought about running. I knew they couldn't catch us but I was afraid we'd get shot.

As we rolled up into balls on the ground we heard, "Hello. What's going on Gus and Wanda? Are my boys bothering you?" It was Dutch. He must've been looking for us.

"Do you know these thieving sneaking boys, Dutch? What'd you let them come over here for anyway? They were going to smash our boys," growled Gus as Wanda shook her ratty hair up and down in agreement waving at their pumpkins.

Dutch was taller and bigger than everybody was but what stood out most was his big smile and friendly voice. He acted like we were just having fun at a picnic dinner or a carnival. Evidently, he didn't see the old man's shotgun and the old lady's leather belt.

"Get up Mickey and Dave and get over here." He said as he chuckled and waved next to his side, "Are you giving Gus and Wanda grief?" We jumped up and ran to his side.

"Wait just minute Dutch, we got damages." These boys smashed our favorite pumpkin, Jack, last night. They're murderers."

"It couldn't have been these two rascals, Gus. They weren't here last night. They were home. I saw them."

"Are you sure?" asked Wanda giving Dutch the evil eye. "We just saw them climbing up Freddie a few minutes ago. Freddie's 20 years old. They would've killed him for sure. They're criminals, and they deserve a whipping," she demanded as she slowly slapped her belt across the palm of her other hand.

"No, we didn't, Dutch. I was getting ready to climb the pumpkin but the shotgun blast scared me so badly I just dropped to the ground."

"That's right," said Dave shaking his head like a jack in the box in agreement.

"There you go, Wanda and Gus. The boys never climbed your boys," as he waved towards the pumpkin patch. "They got too scared to do it." Dutch smiled as he put his hand out to shake hands with Gus, who didn't react to the handshake at all.

"Well, it's been great seeing you both," said Dutch, as he started backing us away.

"Just a minute you snake charmer," chided Wanda as she stepped forward. "What if someone smashes your pumpkins when you aren't here?" she said in a threating tone.

"I'd be upset for sure Wanda but I know I have great neighbors, and they'd never do anything on purpose. So, I wouldn't be mad."

"Well, keep your boys away from our boys and our pumpkin patch, Dutch. 'Cause if you don't somebody's going to get hurt," said Gus as Wanda shook her head in agreement.

"Say you're sorry, boys." We apologized and then the three of us hustled to Dutch's truck. Dave and I climbed in the bed of the truck to drive to the garden and load the vegetables and fruit so we could go home.

Once we finished our work in the garden, and the fire was out, we drove home. Dave and I sat in the cab with Dutch because there wasn't room in the bed.

Dutch never got mad at anybody. He was always happy, but on our way home, he sounded worried. He told us Wanda and Gus were odd people and that we needed to avoid them and their pumpkin patch in the future. He was especially concerned about Gus shooting his gun.

"Don't ever go back there again, Mickey. Do you understand me? They're not just weird, they're dangerous!"

"They're not just dangerous, Dutch, they're witches! Did you see how they dress? She wears that dark cape and that pointy hat. I'll bet she's got a flying broom. And Gus, well, he looks like a doggone scarecrow. He might be a zombie or a mummy or something. And, they said they put a magic spell on some boys and stuck them in those pumpkins. Didn't they, Dave?"

"Yep, they said they could stick us in the pumpkins too. They said they'd eat us too, Dutch. I'm not going back for sure. I don't want to be eaten or jailed in a pumpkin like Jack or Freddie."

Well, Dutch put his head back and roared with laughter all of the way home. He acted like Dave and I were funnier than Jonathan Winters.

"It's true, Dutch. Honest. They're witches for sure, and they got a bunch of boys hidden in those pumpkins. I could see the boys' faces through the pumpkins. I could."

Dutch never stopped laughing all the way home. "You guys have been watching too many Boris Karloff movies. There aren't any witches, mummies or boogeymen. They're just a couple of old crazy people, who caught you climbing on their pumpkins, and they want to scare you away. That's all."

I didn't want to argue with Dutch. He was wrong and too old to believe in monsters that kids knew were real. One night, I felt the Werewolf stalking me when I was walking home from a Boy Scout meeting. I broke into a sweat and ran all of the way home. He would've caught if I hadn't. And, doctors could easily sew a human together like Frankenstein. No problem.

We dropped the whole discussion about witches and bewitched pumpkins. I figured Dave and I could talk about it later without Dutch. It's not Dutch's fault. He's just a grown-up that's all. He can't believe in magic or monsters anymore. He probably doesn't even believe in Santa anymore, but he's still my pal.

&

CHAPTER 5

HELP!

Halloween was definitely a significant holiday. It was bigger than Valentine's Day or July Fourth. Why? Easy peasy. We got pillowcases full of free candy, and we got the day after Halloween off from school for All Saints Day which only required a quick visit to church. What else did we need? As an added bonus, there was lots of holiday hoopla going on for a couple of weeks before Halloween. Kids lived for the holidays during the school year. They were our motivation that kept us doing our homework, science fair projects and studying for spelling bees.

Everybody knew our Halloween anthem and we sang or hummed it everyplace we went. We sang it to the tune of "The Old Gray Mare."

"Great green globs of greasy grimy gopher guts, mutilated monkey meat, dirty, turdy birdie feet.

French fried eyeballs, swimming in a pool of blood, eat it without a spoon. *Burp.*"

Miss Kann loved the holidays as much as we did, maybe more. She had us design our room decorations and bulletin boards weeks before every holiday. For Halloween, Paul and Mike drew scary things that had red blood drawn all over them. They drew bloody skeletons, bloody ghosts, bloody skulls, bloody headstones, bloody rats and ferocious bloody black cats. Then, they pasted their bloody drawings all around the classroom and created a haunted coatroom which was cool; but not really scary.

Mike was especially good at drawing the Boris Karloff, Lon Chaney Jr. and Bella Lugosi movie monsters. He created one bulletin board scene of Frankenstein, Dracula and the Wolfman, all wearing Halloween masks, being led through a cemetery by kids dressed up in Halloween costumes. It looked almost real.

It was so cool it was selected to be painted on the W.T. Grant's store window for a window-painting contest. The contest was sponsored by the businesses along the Rock Road. There were all kinds of neat prizes including a girl's and boy's bike for the grand prizewinners.

On the girls' bulletin board, Kathy, Cindy and Angela used about 500 sheets of colored construction paper to cut out things someone saw in and around a pumpkin patch. None of their cutouts had any blood on them and a white picket fence surrounded the patch. Their pumpkin patch was full of different sizes and shapes of Jack-o'-lanterns that had different faces drawn on them. They connected their pumpkins with green twine which was supposed to be vines. Most of the pumpkins were smiling and none of them were scary. Throughout the pumpkin patch they planted different kinds of trees with fall colored leaves. The girls even used real fall colored leaves and put a small cottage off to the side by the picket fence. None of the guys thought it was scary except me. I liked Paul and Mike's decorations better.

I was obsessed with Gus and Wanda's pumpkins. Every time I looked at the girls' pumpkin patch, I thought about that day with Dave and Dutch at the garden.

I couldn't get Gus and Wanda and their bewitched pumpkins out of my mind. Every pumpkin I sold from my wagon, and every Jack-o'-lantern I saw carved made me think about their boys. Every night I had the same creepy dream about real-life boys being put under a magical spell by Wanda and Gus and stuck into giant pumpkins forever. I knew they were witches and I felt it was up to me to release those boys from their pumpkins.

Halloween was magical for kids and adults that remembered how to be kids. For Halloween, we pretended to be somebody different than a regular kid who went to school, studied and did boring stuff like homework. On Halloween, we were anybody we wanted to be. Monsters. Superheroes. Mad scientists. Zombies.

Anybody. We spent all year imagining cool costumes and testing jokes and tricks to go Trick or Treating for one night to collect pounds of free candy.

We were never surprised when we walked down the street, along the creek or across a ball field and someone shouted out something like, "Killer doctors named Dr. Kill'em and Dr. Catch'em." Instinctively, we debated the merits of the newest costume idea and came up with ideas for how to create the costume. It was fun and we did it all year.

The kids in my class were too old to dress up in store-bought costumes. We dressed up in store-bought costumes like Mighty Mouse and Snow White when were little kids. We had graduated to homemade costumes like hobos, scary creature-like monsters, ghosts and cowboys. This year we wanted to dress up differently from everyone else. The idea I liked best was dressing up like the Beatles but I couldn't get three other guys to agree. Finally, I decided to dress up like a hobo. I didn't know how Joey was dressing up for Halloween because we weren't going together this year. He was going with his friends, and I was going with mine.

During the last couple of weeks, we'd been reading Washington Irving's "The Legend of Sleepy Hollow" in class. At home, I was reading parts of Joey's library copy of Mary Shelley's "Frankenstein." I had nightmares every night.

"Come on, Jim. We'll be safe."

"No, we won't, Mickey. If it was safe Dave would be here, and he's not here."

"Dave's just a scaredy-cat, Jim. You're really brave," I gushed as I tried to pump up his confidence. We were biking down the Rock Road to Gus and Wanda's house in the dark on Halloween night. Truth be told, I was scared too, and I wouldn't have gone alone. I was glad Jim was with me.

I prayed we could break the unholy spell Gus and Wanda had cast on those boys in the giant pumpkins and rescue them. I wasn't sure how but Halloween or as the nuns said, "All Saint's Eve," seemed the perfect time to chant some magical incantations like Open Sesame, Abracadabra or Hail Marys if all else failed. I was determined to save those boys from being stuck in a pumpkin for eternity.

Above us, the Hunter's blue full moon hung ominously. It looked like a big white melmac dinner plate hanging over the GrandPa Pidgeon's store which we were passing. We were cruising along the gravel shoulder on our bikes careful to avoid the potholes and litter especially the shards of broken glass. GrandPa's wasn't busy tonight. It was Halloween and the glare from its parking lot lights helped us peer a little farther into the dark night. It was hard to see well because there weren't any street lights along the Rock Road. The only lights were our Boy Scout flashlights, which we had taped to our handlebars and the full Hunter's moon.

"This is nuts, Mickey," shouted Jim, angry he had come along. "What're we going to do when we get there? We're missing out on all of the free candy tonight."

I winced at the thought. We were giving up a lot to help the entrapped boys escape those pumpkins. Trick or Treating on Halloween was like having the keys to the doors of Kroger or Rexall Drug Store.

All we had to do was show up dressed in a costume and run at lightning speed to as many neighbors' doorways as we could by 9:00 p.m. At each house, we had to tell a quick joke and politely accept a piece of candy or in some cases a whole nickel candy bar. Some houses gave away apples or toothbrushes. We'd just say no thanks and quickly run to the next house. Apples weighed too much and we had plenty at home. If people didn't give out anything, sometimes we'd use a bar of soap on their car windows to write something like "cheap" or "Kilroy was here."

Our parents made us throw away candy that was opened or homemade like popcorn balls. There were always weird stories about kids eating broken glass or rat poison. We ate those things before we got home.

Some of my favorite Halloween treats were wax candy. My favorites were the licorice-flavored black mustache or cherry-flavored reds lips. I'd wear them like a mini-costume. Later, when I got bored, I chewed them until all of the flavor was gone. When all I had left was a wad of wax in my mouth, I'd spit it out first chance into a trash can.

"We can buy candy later. Tonight, we're going to save those boys in the pumpkins."

"How, Mickey?"

"We'll know what to do when we get there. Trust me."

"Yeah sure," mumbled Jim as we turned onto Mo Bottom Road. I didn't tell Jim that one of the older guys told me Mo Bottom Road was nicknamed "Zombie Road" because lots of people had been killed on it over the years. Supposedly at night you could see ghosts and floating bubble-like globes. I prayed we wouldn't see any.

We ditched our bikes under a brush pile at Dutch's garden which worried Jim. He was riding his brother's bike. After we made sure our bikes were well covered with vines, corn stalks and tomato plants, we quietly skulked toward Gus' and Wanda's pumpkin patch through the fields. We never spoke louder than a whisper. I warned Jim about Gus's shotgun and how he threatened to shoot us if we came back to hurt his boys.

The bright eerie moon cast a dull white glow over everything in the farm fields, and it helped us see where we were going. We avoided the few houses along the way. We didn't turn on our flashlights in case someone saw them. We walked and crawled in a zigzag pattern from brush piles, to a tractor and then to a barn like we had seen in John Wayne Army movies. We were slowly getting closer and closer to the haunted pumpkin patch.

It was scary to hear the night sounds out in the country. It was like our Boy Scout campouts without a hundred guys yacking it up. We heard dogs barking off in the distance, owls hooting in the trees and some kind of screeching bird overhead. It sounded like the mysterious bird was spying on us.

Silently, we crawled around the corner of a corrugated metal shed. We were startled when we suddenly came face to face with a mother deer and her doe. We all froze, blinked, and looked back and forth at each other. As suddenly as we saw them, they disappeared like ghosts into the soft breeze without a sound. They stunned us, and we needed a moment to catch our breath before we tiptoed away.

What if it had been Gus and his shotgun instead of a deer and a doe? We would have been shot dead right now. We were creeped out, and it took some convincing to keep Jim from bolting.

Across a large cornfield full of dead stalks, where the deer had run, the moonlight reflected off Gus's and Wanda's house. Behind their home, we saw a large brightly burning bonfire that reflected enough firelight to make the gigantic orange pumpkins glow as they laid in the patch. It looked freaky as a cool breeze sent a shiver up our backs. We both felt afraid.

"What're we going to do now, Sherlock? We're crazy, Mickey. You're going to get us shot. Let's go home and get some candy. There's still time," whispered Jim.

Swallowing hard and feeling hot and sweaty on a chilly fall night, I urged us towards the patch. "We're going to be fine, Jim. We need to help those guys trapped in the pumpkins. Trust me."

"Yeah sure. Who're you the Texaco Man with the star?" moaned Jim as we belly crawled closer and closer through the dead cornstalks toward the glowing pumpkin patch.

"We'll be fine," I lied as we got our first good look at their house and the pumpkin patch. "Look at that bonfire. It's really blazing. Why are there so many cars at their house?" I whispered, pointing at the parked cars.

"It's Halloween night. "There must be more witches. You're right. Something is happening tonight. Let's go get the police. They're witches!" Before I could grab him or say anything, Jim took off half crawling and half-running towards the bikes.

"Wait, Jim," I whispered when I caught up with him. "There's no time to get help before they do something to those guys in the pumpkins. It's up to us. It'll take us more than an hour to get help. We have to do this by ourselves." With that stark realization, we both got a lot more scared. What unholy ritual were they celebrating on All Hallow's Eve during a full moon?

"What if they catch us and put us in a giant pumpkin, Mickey? What'll happen then? Nobody even knows we're out here tonight," stuttered Jim.

"Well, that's the chance we took coming out here tonight," I stuttered back at him. "Let's go," I stammered feeling the cold chill of the night air hit my sweaty body and send a spine-tingling chill right up my spine. We crawled through the field toward the gigantic glowing pumpkins.

The closer we crawled, the more aware our senses became. The bloodcurdling sounds were getting louder and louder. We heard women screaming and wolves barking and howling. Deep eerie laughs stopped us dead in our tracks yet dared us to keep crawling toward the pumpkin patch.

When we arrived at the edge of the pumpkin patch, we hid among the shadows and cornstalks. There weren't ordinary people like us standing around the bonfire. There were dozens of witches, vampires, goblins and ghosts chatting and laughing as they stood around it. Directly in front of us was the back of the tallest person I had ever seen. He was standing next to a wolf standing on its hind legs. All of the monsters were staring at the bonfire whose flames shot at least 30 feet in the air. The fire released sparks and embers that flew even higher.

The bonfire was so large and bright we could hear it suck the oxygen out of the cold night air. Its roiling flames reflected onto the mammoth pumpkins. The reflections from the dancing flames on to the pumpkins made them look like they were alive. It could have been a surreal scene from the "Abbott and Costello Meet Frankenstein" movie.

Our unblinking eyes were as big as golf balls as we watched Gus and Wanda promenade out of their cottage. They were hand-in-hand as they walked toward the bonfire to the loud applause from everyone around the fire.

When they reached hell's fire, Gus threw something into it that magically caused its flames to shoot even higher and turn a bright red. As the fire burned red hot, the song "Monster Mash" started to play loudly and everyone started dancing. It was a Monster Ball.

The eerie Halloween party for all of their monstrous friends was in full swing. It looked like a creepy good time as long as you weren't one of the oversize pumpkins that was standing sentinel over the party or us.

The faint faces on the glowing iridescent, orange pumpkins mesmerized me. It looked like their eyes were blinking and their mouths were moving. They were actually talking to Gus and Wanda. It was the scariest thing I ever witnessed including every late-night horror movie I ever watched.

Fear. We've all felt it. It makes our teeth chatter; our hearts pound, and our knees knock. Fear. It makes us break into a cold sweat and stutter. We closed our eyes and held our ears but our fear wouldn't go away. Jim and I were frozen with fear.

Fear. You've probably watched a black and white Count Dracula movie late at night in your basement and were afraid to walk up the stairs by yourself in the dark. Fear. Remember the night when you saw a silhouette in the darkness? Was it a ghost across the room spying on you? Fear. I remember the wet foggy night I walked home through the schoolyard after watching a Werewolf movie at Tommy's. I could feel someone or something in the tree-tops waiting to jump on me. So, I didn't walk under any trees all of the way home. Fear is real. It's palpable. You can even taste it.

That's the sweat inducing fear we felt when a skeleton shockingly stood up in its coffin right in front of us and started dancing. It was looking right through our souls.

I wasn't sure what followed next. Did my hair stand straight up on end first or did Jim jump up slap his hands to his cheeks and start banshee screaming so loudly everyone heard him? No matter. Everyone turned toward us and gave us their evil eyes even the pumpkins. The skeleton threw one of his eyeballs, and it hit me hard right in the middle of my forehead. Nothing is ever more horrifying until it is. In unison, every monster within what seemed like a thousand miles started running towards us. And yes, Frankenstein and the Wolf Man were standing in front of us at the fire. Fear. Heart-stopping and bloodcurdling fear froze our hearts and our feet in place.

Before we could blink, all of the ghosts, vampires, goblins and witches overwhelmed us. All we could do was scream for help as loud as we could. We were trapped and captured.

That's when Mom shook me awake.

"Wake up, Mickey. Wake up. What are you dreaming about?" she whispered. When I opened my eyes, everybody was standing around my bed staring at me through their grumpy and red-rimmed sleep-deprived eyes.

"Jim and I were being chased by a bunch of monsters even Frankenstein and the Wolf Man. We were trying to save those boys from the pumpkins. They were going to put us under a spell and put us in pumpkins too," I said breathlessly, as I rubbed the sleep out of my eyes. My bed and my pajamas were completely soaked with sweat.

"Boo," said Joey making a gesture like he was going to grab me. "You guys shouldn't let Mickey go Trick or Treating tonight because he woke us up. Go to sleep, punk," said Joey as he stalked back to bed.

"Goodnight, Mickey, kisses and hugs," said Mom as she gently hugged my shoulders. "You just had a bad nightmare. You shouldn't watch those scary movies." Dad grumbled something over his shoulder as he went back to bed.

As I laid in bed, trying to forget my dream, I rolled the rubber ball that looked like an eyeball in my hand. I had won it for coming in third place in the Spelling Bee. Shuddering, I decided I was going Trick or Treating instead of to the pumpkin patch for Halloween.

The next pumpkin I wanted to see was in a Thanksgiving pumpkin pie.

❧

CHAPTER 6

ALL THINGS MUST PASS

"It's true! It's true! The crown has made it clear.
The climate must be perfect all the year.

The law was made a distant moon ago here:
July and August cannot be too hot.

And there's a legal limit to the snow here
in Camelot.

The winter is forbidden till December,
And exits March the second on the dot.

By order, summer lingers through September
in Camelot.

Camelot! Camelot!
I know it sounds a bit bizarre,

But in Camelot, Camelot
That's how conditions are.

The rain may never fall till after sundown.
By eight, the morning fog must disappear.
In short, there's simply not
A more congenial spot
For happily-ever-aftering than here
in Camelot.

Camelot! Camelot!

I know it gives a person pause,
But in Camelot, Camelot
Those are the legal laws.

The snow may never slush upon the hillside.
By nine p.m. the moonlight must appear.
In short, there's simply not
A more congenial spot
For happily-ever-aftering than here in Camelot."

Lyrics from Camelot by Alan Jay Lerner

We called the good ol' USA Camelot when John Fitzgerald
Kennedy was president. Tragically, Camelot died at 1:00 p.m.

on Friday, November 22, 1963. Every American, over the age of seven, knew precisely where they were when they heard President Kennedy had been shot and was dead.

I was kneeling on the shiny, red and black hard asbestos tile floor in my classroom saying a rosary with my classmates for his safety. We knew he had been shot. After we heard he died, we prayed for his eternal salvation. The whole time I thought about how badly my knees ached from kneeling on the hard tile floor. Prayers were said in every classroom in St. Kevin, and I'm sure every other classroom and church around the country. We were wretchedly sad.

President Kennedy was our King Arthur, and Mrs. Kennedy was our Queen Guinevere. The Kennedys were our Irish royalty. We lived our lives watching their glamorous lives unfold on the evening news, in pictorial magazines and in the daily morning and evening newspapers. Kids never heard the whispers of the darker side of Camelot and most parents ignored what they heard.

America hadn't had royalty since Franklin Delano Roosevelt was president. The Roosevelts weren't a young, hip, Hollywood-glamorous couple like the Kennedys even though they helped save Western Europe and Asia. The Roosevelts were plain and somewhat homely except for his aristocratic Pince-nez glasses and long slender cigarette holder.

The Kennedys were svelte and fashionable. They were shown in chic tuxedos and elegant gowns or windswept on a sailboat with stylish sunglasses and their trendy hair blowing in the wind. President Kennedy did more for Harvard than Harvard did for him. Everyone loved to listen to his Massachusetts accent so much they bought and listened to five million copies of Vaughn Meader's "The First Family" comedy album.

In fact, a lot of us did a reasonably good impression of the President saying, "Ask not what your country can do for you, ask what you can do for your country." It was a ready joke, and it always brought a smile. People substituted nouns, pronouns or names, like mom or Mickey for the word country.

Americans spent two and a half years obsessed with watching the Kennedys stumble through Equal Rights demonstrations, union boss investigations and the Bay of Pigs. When Kennedy had a convincing win with the Cuban Missile Crisis, everybody cheered. A majority of Americans, especially Catholics, prayed he'd be re-elected.

Kennedy's assassination gave a reason to instantaneously bestow immortal status and prompt thousands of streets and schools to be named in his honor. Many people compared President Kennedy to President Lincoln, a homely president who saved the nation during his presidency. We didn't care. No matter what he did or didn't do as president, we loved King John and his endearing royal family, Queen Jacqueline, Princess Caroline and Prince John-John. The country had been previously devastated when baby Prince Patrick died.

Even Dad felt wretched about President Kennedy's death, and he had voted for Richard Nixon. Americans felt somehow responsible for his assassination. We felt we had failed as a nation to protect our president.

We got out of school early once we finished the rosary. When I got home, Mom was sitting on the sofa with her teary red-rimmed blue eyes glued to our modern "portable" black and white TV. She was watching Walter Cronkite, the most trusted man in America, report on the late-breaking news stories that surrounded the ghastly assassination. There was another tragedy about a Dallas policeman named J.D. Tippit. He was shot and killed about 45 minutes after Kennedy.

Mom learned every detail as Walter Cronkite reported them on TV through his misty eyes and thick black plastic glasses. Later, when Dad got home from work, Mom and Dad sat together on the couch mesmerized and depressed. It was like a death in our family. Mom couldn't even fix dinner. They sat there for the next four days watching and re-watching the same news stories surrounding the assassination, President Johnson's swearing-in and old film clips of the Kennedy clan on vacation sailing and playing football at the family compound. Camelot was dead.

Mom and Dad also watched the real-time assassination of Lee Harvey Oswald by Jack Ruby. Afterward, all three of the network TV stations, ABC, NBC and CBS showed the Oswald assassination repeatedly, and in slow motion, from morning until the Indian chief's face came on at midnight and the airwaves shut down.

It was unbearable to watch the public pass by Kennedy's casket in the Rotunda for two days, and then watch the black stallion without a rider prance in the funeral procession. The stallion represented the President at the head of the long torturous funeral procession down Pennsylvania Avenue. It was more than Mom could bear when John-John saluted his father's flag-draped casket. She wept uncontrollably. It was indeed the death of Camelot and our dear King Arthur. The world was changing in ways that couldn't be calculated at that time.

During that weekend, Mom and Dad watched more TV than Joey and I were allowed to watch in three weeks. Once, I changed the TV channel when Mom went to the bathroom but the other two network stations were airing the same stories. Grief-stricken, we were trapped in our American TV tragedy.

Joey and I were limited to an hour of the "idiot box" at night after we did our homework. The only way we got to watch TV on Saturday before our chores were done was to wake up really early before Mom and Dad. If we did, we could watch the Three Stooges or the Little Rascals before they woke up but not the weekend President Kennedy died. If they weren't watching the news about the assassination, they were in church praying.

America was plummeting into a profound depression, and the continuous TV coverage made everyone who watched it even more depressed. How could such a heinous crime happen in America? We were the leaders of the free world. Many thought it was Nikita Khrushchev and the Soviet Union Communists who killed President Kennedy. Why did Jack Ruby, the owner of a nightclub, assassinate Lee Harvey Oswald, a suspected Communist sympathizer? Did Oswald shoot President Kennedy? He claimed he didn't. Why would he? Who shot Officer Tippit? Why? Was it really the Russians or some other plot far more sinister like the CIA or FBI? Those types of questions haunted every American and all of the adults who had a TV watched them like they were crystal balls to find the answers to the questions. No one had the answers and everyone became even more obsessed with the Kennedys. Americans bought and saved every magazine or newspaper that had any news about the Kennedys and the assassination.

Although my friends and I were sad, we were bored sitting at home. We took to the cold outdoors to explore. We only went home when we had to eat. Mom and Dad took little interest in what we were doing. So, we took advantage of the tragedy and expanded our territory to the unexplored world surrounding us.

Larry suggested we explore a rust bucket junkyard he had seen along Adie Road. All we needed to get excited about the new adventure was to hear the junkyard had warning signs posted about dogs that would kill us if we trespassed. Of course, we didn't believe the signs. Who owned killer dogs in St. Ann?

As we crept through the junkyard, we saw abandoned and rusted cars, trucks and old construction equipment. It felt like we were walking through an iron graveyard. Most of the vehicles were missing fenders, headlights, seats, windshields or other things that were salvageable. Dads fixed everything that could be fixed. The colors were oxidized and faded. A lot of the rubber tires were gone too. I saw old sedans, pick-up trucks, station wagons and coupes. Most of the cars were totally smashed and wrecked. Some were just old and worn out. None of them were shiny or even almost new.

The junked cars must have driven families to work and to church until they just fell apart. An old red and white early 50s Ford station wagon had two holes in its windshield where it looked like heads had gone through it. I shuddered and wondered if someone was killed. Besides us sneaking through the junkyard, it was as quiet as a cemetery.

Just as we clambered over the top of a rickety old wooden and wire fence to get out of the junkyard, four huge furry, slobbering, growling and barking dogs lunged at the fence. Luckily, they knocked us over the fence instead of knocking us back into the junkyard. They were so big they almost knocked the fence down when they lunged at us. Knocked to the ground and shaken, we stood up and brushed the dust off our jeans. As we made faces and barked at them, they viciously and repeatedly attacked the fence. Slobber fell from their snarling mouths.

"I guess they do have killer dogs," stuttered Larry. "I thought their sign was a joke. We sure got lucky."

As we backed away from the dogs and the wobbly fence, some man screamed at them to shut up and called them home. I guess he thought we were some rabbits or raccoons.

As we turned away, we barely saw the road. It was a hard-to-see, overgrown, weedy lane that opened to the Rock Road right next to the junkyard fence. None of us had ever seen it before. I had walked or ridden past it dozens of times. The shady lane looked creepy. It made me think about Gus and Wanda. What were we going to find if we ventured up the lane?

"Let's go up there, you guys. It's another adventure," suggested Larry.

"We should go home, you guys. We're going to get shot or eaten by wild dogs. Look what happened to President Kennedy," countered Dave.

"Aw don't be a scaredy-cat, Dave. My dad said the Communists shot Kennedy. We'll be in the woods. Nobody even knows this road exists," mocked Larry.

"Oh sure, Larry. Nobody knows. Sure. Who do you think built it? Ghosts?" smirked Dave.

"Why don't we walk up, and see what we see. Okay, Dave?" I suggested, hoping Dave wanted to stay out and have some fun. The junkyard dogs and Kennedy's assassination had him wound tighter than an alarm clock.

Grudgingly, he agreed and we slowly trekked up the lane. We were careful not to let anybody see us. We stayed on the lane and out of the woods. We didn't want to get those brown sticky weed seeds on our clothes. There were always thousands of them and they were impossible to peel off your clothes and shoes.

The trees that lined the winding gravel lane had lost their leaves. Walking along, we kicked the brown, yellow, orange and red leaves that were about a foot deep. We were all a little nervous, but we acted brave. None of us talked.

I didn't want to run into some madman like Gus or a cop. As we got further up the hill, we heard some kids' voices off in the distance. They were yelling but we didn't understand what they were saying.

"We should go home, you guys. This isn't going to end well," implored Dave.

"No, let's stay. We can get off this road and get into the woods. We can sneak up on those guys and see what they're doing," challenged Larry as he stuck out his chin and crossed his arms, daring us to be as brave as him.

They both looked at me to decide. I thought a minute about my experiences over the last month and was ready to leave with Dave when Larry called us chicken.

"Why would you call us chicken?" I asked Larry. "We're not anymore scared than you are right now."

"I'm not scared," declared Larry holding his arms crossed and daring us.

"Bull," said Dave walking down the lane. 'Why don't you go up there by yourself and Mickey and I will go home since you aren't scared." Larry begged us to stay.

"C'mon guys! It's a new adventure. Imagine what the guys will say when we tell them about this place. We'll be heroes."

"Look at Kennedy; he's a hero, and he's dead," said Dave.

"Well, let's just keep walking and stay really low so we can't be seen. As soon as we see someone or something that we don't like, we'll turn around and run home. Okay?" pleaded Larry.

"Well, you better take it back that we're scared or I'm not going."

"Yeah, me either," I agreed, and Larry quickly took back his insults. We started walking again and listened for the voices which had faded out of our hearing.

"Who do you think that was?" asked Larry.

"I don't know, but you better hope it's not a murderer or a monster Larry because Mickey and I are faster than you," chuckled Dave. Larry stopped when he realized what Dave had said.

When we got to the top of the long and winding road, we saw an actual farm. There was a large slightly dilapidated, red faded wooden barn on our left. Straight ahead was the farmhouse. The house was weathered and larger than the homes in St. Ann. It was a faded white three-story house with a round turret on its corner. We didn't hear any voices, as Larry ran towards the barn waving for us to follow him. We were alert and cautious.

"Do you think anybody lives here except ghosts? The whole place looks haunted to me," said Dave as we crawled to the back of the barn staying in the shadows. There was an open door on the backside of the barn. Inside looked eerie. We smelled hay, dust, dirt and wood. A half dozen wooden animal stalls lined one wall. An old tractor and other farm stuff like shovels, pitchforks and a rusty wheelbarrow were spread around. There weren't any animals but it definitely looked like someone, maybe even ghosts, were living here. We saw haystacks in the loft as Larry climbed up the wooden ladder to look around. We followed him careful not to trip as we all sneezed from the hay and dust floating in the air.

We had never seen anything like this haunted farm before. Larry whispered, "Hey guys, this is a gable barn."

"What?" I asked.

"A gable barn is the kind of barn it is, Mickey. You know I want to be an architect. Well, Dad stops when we're driving, and he sees different kinds of barns. This is a gable barn."

"It's more like a haunted barn," said Dave to no one in particular, as Larry crawled not so carefully or quietly across the hayloft to the loft door in the front of the barn. It was wide open and slowly squeaking back and forth in the wind. Silently, we followed him. It was a spectacular view. We were higher than most of the treetops, and for a moment, I felt like a bird flying. We could see the entire deserted farm and the woods surrounding it below.

It looked like a scene from "The Twilight Zone." I was expecting to hear Rod Serling say, "Time was frozen in a moment long ago before we were even born." We didn't see or hear anybody or anything except the frosty fall wind blowing the loft door. Many smaller farm buildings were surrounding the barn beside the Victorian mansion.

"Wow, this is creepy, guys," I said. "It's like space aliens sucked everybody up into their space ship all in the same instant. Nobody must've survived. If they did somebody would be here."

"Let's get out of here. I don't want to be a dead hero," said Dave.

Larry and I climbed down from the loft and ran outside to check out all of the deserted buildings.

"Chicken," called Larry over his shoulder as he ran over to a one-story grey weathered wooden building. It had a wire fenced yard on its side.

"I'll bet this is a chicken coop," said Larry.

He was right. Inside, we saw feathers lying around and about twenty wooden nesting baskets that were still lined in hay. It looked like a flock of chickens would squawk and walk in any moment. Everything was pretty much in place except somebody had thrown some wire baskets around.

When we tried to walk back outside of the coop, we couldn't open the door. It was locked. "Hey Dave, open the darn door."

"Say you're a big yellow chicken turd Larry or I'll never let you out," said Dave. We looked out a small window in the chicken coop. Dave was sitting on the top wooden rail of a corral for cows and horses. He was chewing on a piece of hay and looked like he was on the set of 'Rawhide.'

"Not on your life," yelled Larry. "Open the door, you jerk."

"Say you're a big yellow chicken turd and I will, Larry."

"Just say it, Larry. He's not going to let us out otherwise. I don't want to break a window or the door. It's too cool."

"Okay Dave, I'm a big yellow chicken turd, and you're a big jerk that can't take a joke."

With a big smile, Dave unlocked the door to the chicken coop.

"What's that place?" asked Larry pointing as he ran to a low, long and narrow one-story brick building behind the coop. It had windows and a door. It looked locked but the door opened when he turned the knob. Inside was completely empty, and it had a concrete floor with a drain. We couldn't figure out what it was. "Maybe it's a tool shed," offered Dave.

There were several other buildings around the farm. The coolest was a brick silo that was at least thirty feet tall with vines growing up its side. One was a shed where it looked like they cut wood and kept it dry. Another was made out of logs, and it looked like they only used half the logs it needed. "I think this is where they dried tobacco and seed," said Larry. Another building looked like it was used to smoke meat. It faintly smelled like meat was cooking inside.

As we walked outside into the fresh air, we looked up a path that led to a big wrap around front porch on the gigantic weathered white house with a green roof. Drawn like magnets, we raced to see who got to the front door first. "I win," I said out of breath.

More cautious than we had been, we crept inside not knowing what to expect. The house was intact except there wasn't any furniture, rugs or pictures hanging on the wall. There were ghost-like rectangular shapes on the walls where it looked like pictures had been hanging for a 100-years but the pictures were gone. The house was empty. It seemed sad and unhappy as the wind whistled through its open windows. It sounded like it was breathing.

As the wooden screen door slammed closed behind us, it felt like the house wanted a bunch of laughing kids and hardworking parents tramping loudly and lovingly through the front door. The house seemed happy we had come for a visit.

We tiptoed throughout the large rambling house afraid of stirring up any old ghosts or rats who lived there. As we walked throughout the house, we tried to guess how each room was used and who slept where. We looked out every window to make sure everything was real and that we didn't imagine things. We were happy we didn't see anybody.

We ended up in the attic. To be truthful, it took courage to walk into a dark and dank attic that smelled like mold. Luckily, there was a small hole in the roof that shed some sunlight to see. That's when we saw it.

It was a large trunk that looked like a pirate's chest sitting in the corner of the attic all by itself.

"Holy cow! I hope that's what I think it is because I think it's a treasure chest," crowed Larry as he ran to the chest ready to open it.

"Don't open it," ordered Dave quite seriously. "It feels haunted to me. It might have dead souls or something awful in it. Let's leave it and get out of here you guys. This place is haunted. Can't you feel it?"

"It feels haunted to me too, Dave. We're lucky it's daytime."

"This is so cool! We can't tell anybody, okay? It'll just be our personal playground. Don't ever bring anybody else here. Okay?" pleaded Larry.

Then Larry opened the chest, looked inside and screamed like a banshee. When he shouted, Dave ran out of the attic so fast I felt his breeze as he passed me.

"What is it," I asked looking inside as Larry laughed.

"I don't know it's too dark to see," said Larry. "Don't move it Mickey until I go outside and find Dave."

Realizing I was in the dark attic of a haunted house, alone, and that someone's head might be inside the trunk. I wanted to bolt but something stopped me. Instead, I pulled the chest over to the shaft of sunlight from the roof and looked inside. It was full of old black and white photos. They told the story of a family. There were old wedding photos, photos of babies and photos of the same family at different times in their lives. The coolest photo was one of a group of men building the house where I was standing. One man was working on the roof right about where I was standing. What happened? Everyone was gone now. After looking for a few more minutes, it was feeling creepy in the attic. The guys never came back. So, I closed the trunk and pushed it over to the corner where we found it.

The sunlight in the rooms felt warm after being in the dark attic. Quietly, I crept back through the house wondering what had happened to Dave and Larry. I didn't hear them. As I walked, I tried to imagine what it must've been like to live with the family on the farm growing up. In the kitchen, somebody jumped out of the pantry behind me and yelled at the top of his lungs.

Shaken, I reflexively jumped and screamed at the top of my lungs and bolted through the kitchen door to the porch. Outside, Joey and Greg were standing with Dave and Larry. Everybody was laughing and pointing at me.

"What are you scared of, Suzie?" yelled Billy as he chased me through the kitchen door letting the screen door slam shut. "Are you scared of ghosts?"

"No, I'm scared of your big ugly face, Billy. You're a jerk," I yelled. I must've looked scared. Even Dave and Larry were laughing.

After everybody quit laughing, we lounged around on the porch and exchanged stories about the farm. Joey and his friends had been coming to the farm for a couple of weeks. They told us how they caught Butch and Booger putting the shed on fire and how they called the fire department to get them in trouble. Butch and Booger hadn't come back since.

The older guys told us about a unique way they played capture the flag and challenged us. We accepted.

We spent the rest of the day hiding our rag flags in the best hiding spots on the farm that we could find. The rules were simple. We had to hang our banners somewhere that they could be seen from the ground. We couldn't hide them under something or in a hole.

The second rule hurt sometimes. We didn't have to physically tag the guy on the other team to put them in jail. We could also tag the guy with a roof shingle that we sailed through the air like a Wham-O Frisbee. Getting "tagged" by a six-inch square of asphalt roof shingle soaring through the air at the speed of sound—hurt. We tried not to hit each other above the shoulders. Of course, some of us threw better than others.

The games started us against them but as the day wore on we mixed up the teams, so we didn't get bored. It was like before we quit hanging out together for Joey and me. It was like we were never mad at each other. We were laughing and joking with each other like we did before the Jamboree.

One time, I was chasing Joey by the silo to tag him with a tile when he suddenly face-planted into the ground. Worried about him falling, I didn't throw my roof tile at him. Instead, I ran up to him and stooped down to see if he was okay.

"Are you okay, Joey?" I asked as he tagged me and yelled, "Sucker. You're in jail."

Disappointed that he had outsmarted me, I watched him stand up and walk. He had a bad limp as he walked me to the chicken coop which was his team's jail. Joey limped the rest of the day. When I asked him if he was okay, he told me to mind my own business. So, I did.

We ran, played, yelled and argued all day, and the house and farm seemed happy. When the sun set behind the house and we were leaving everyone, including the farm, looked sad.

I walked next to Joey, who was still limping, down the gravel driveway. Everybody was tired but we were bragging about throws and moves we had made on the other guys all afternoon. It was a great day, and everything was fine between Joey and me.

"Are you okay, Joey," I asked.

"Yeah, I'm fine, but you won't be if you ask me again." I smiled, and he smiled back.

As the guys peeled off at various intersections named after saints to go home, we'd smile, hurl an insult and say goodbye. We knew we had shared a special day together. Sadly, one of the best days of my life was over.

I had forgotten about President Kennedy until I saw Mom and Dad sitting on the sofa still watching our black and white TV. My smile faded as I thought about our friend Allen who had drowned last summer. I'm not sure why I thought about Allen as Joey limped and I walked to the kitchen to grab an apple since Mom hadn't started dinner yet.

The only upside from President Kennedy's death was that every place, including St. Kevin, was closed on Monday for his funeral. Although we were happy to get an extra day off from school, the grown-ups were pre-occupied with the pageantry of the President's spectacular funeral. The country was grieving.

With the pall of the funeral, how was it going to affect Thanksgiving? I didn't see how it was going to be as much fun this year as it had been in the past at Grandma's house. At her home, all of our cousins came for a huge family celebration. This past year, two families of cousins had moved. One moved to New York City and the other moved to Nashville. So, everyone living in

St. Louis was coming to our house for Thanksgiving. The whole weekend reminded me of a saying my Gigi would say, "This too shall pass," and it did.

CHAPTER 7

WITH A LITTLE HELP FROM MY FRIENDS

Every family has at least one. You know whom I'm talking about, the grouch. Ours was Great-Uncle Albert. He was old, mostly blind, always gloomy and smelled like dust and stinky cigars. He was always dressed in the same old rumpled navy-blue suit with a wrinkled white shirt and a stained black tie. He wore a beat-up gray homburg, green sunglasses and he shuffled with a white cane. Mom and Dad felt sorry for him because he lived alone. I felt sorry for us because we had to spend time with him during the holidays. I also felt guilty, so I tried to act pleasant and helpful.

He got married when he came back from World War I but his young wife and unborn first child died from scarlet fever. None of us knew her but he carried a small photo of her in a locket that he kept on a pocket watch chain he kept in his vest pocket. He didn't like kids except when he needed us to fetch stuff for him. He never said please or thank you. He mostly knew how to sit down and get in everyone's way. So, we had to walk around him.

Dad said, Grandpa said, losing his wife and being in the War changed Uncle Albert. Kids don't know what really happens in real wars. We only know what happens in John Wayne war movies. I wanted was an uncle that was fun to be around, and Uncle Albert wasn't any fun. He rarely laughed at funny jokes but if we dropped a dish and it broke, or we stubbed our toe, he'd chuckle until tears ran down his cheek. He didn't talk much. He never asked how we were doing or went to our ball games. He was a grouch so that's what we called him behind his back, Uncle Grouch.

Dad asked me to drive with him to pick up Uncle Grouch to bring him to our house for Thanksgiving dinner. Joey wasn't going with us because both of his legs were hurting now. I figured he was faking. I got stuck going with Dad to pick up the Grouch.

Dad also wanted to visit Grandpa's gravesite in Calvary Cemetery. Grandpa and Uncle Albert were brothers. I barely knew Grandpa. He died before I went to school. I remember he had a loud laugh, a broad smile and gave me presents for my birthday and Christmas. I never understood how Grandpa had a brother like Uncle Grouch.

When we got to the Grouch's house, I got a big surprise. "Here, boy," he said, as he pointed to a pile of stuff on his floor by the door.

"What are they?" I asked, looking at the stained cardboard box and an intriguing silver metal suitcase.

"They're things I picked up during my travels," he said as he almost smiled. Uncle Albert had been an over-the-road "big rig" truck driver before his eyesight went bad. He drove between St. Louis and Los Angeles when Route 66 was a two-lane highway. He traveled throughout California too.

First, I opened the metal suitcase. It was jammed full. Half of it was full of hundreds of neatly organized round 3D View-Master slide wheels. The other half held what looked like hundreds of postcards. When I looked up at Uncle Albert, I was sure he was smiling at me. I tried to smile back. "Thanks a lot, Uncle Albert," I mumbled. Not sure what else to say, I looked back into the suitcase and pulled one of each out. They smelled like cigars.

The postcard unfolded into seven different colorful photographs of the Sierra Nevada Mountains. I tried to look at the small wheel of photos, but there wasn't a viewer. "Look in the cardboard box, Mickey," said Uncle Albert. I was stunned as I looked at him. He and Dad were definitely smiling. Shoot, I didn't even know the Grouch knew my name.

I dug into the cardboard box. Inside were a View-Master and a View-Master projector for the slides.

"Put it into the View-Master Mickey so you can see," said Uncle Albert smiling broadly. I collected these things when I was driving over the road to California. I loved that place."

"What do you say, Mickey?" pleaded Dad.

"Huh, oh thanks, Uncle Albert. These are really cool," I said, but I didn't really mean. I quickly clicked through a wheel of color photos of Southern California wildflowers.

"You're welcome. I'm sure you and Joey will love looking at the View-Masters and postcards as much as I did when I could see better. I figured I'd give them to you boys now. I hope you travel to California someday, Mickey. It's different than St. Louis. It's beautiful! I should've stayed," said Uncle Albert wistfully looking up at the dingy, smoke-stained white ceiling of his small bungalow on Penrose Avenue in North St. Louis.

I really didn't know what to say to him. I didn't even know the Grouch knew our names. He never called us by our names before. He just called us "boy" like "Not you, boy, the other boy," and he'd never given us a gift. I wasn't sure these things actually qualified as gifts though since they weren't new and they smelled like cigars. I felt a pang of guilt looking into the suitcase full of his memories. He seemed so happy as he remembered his travels.

I felt embarrassed for feeling so ungrateful and promised myself to spend some time looking at them someday.

"Give Uncle Albert a hug to say thanks," said Dad coaxing me to get up and walk over to him.

"Oh, he's too big to hug me," said Uncle Albert clutching his white cane with both hands. "We can just shake hands like gentlemen."

Relieved, I stood up, walked over to him, looked straight into his green sunglasses and shook hands. We were both smiling but I wasn't sure we meant it.

After the cemetery, on our way home, I was shivering in the back seat of the car. I kept my window open and my head down because of all the cigar smoke. The smoke hung over our heads like a rain cloud.

Seeing Grandpa's and Grandma's headstones at the cemetery wasn't too sad for me. I didn't know them well. I did wonder what they were like and if we would've had fun together. I would've been gravely sad if it was my Grandma, Mom's mom. She was my best friend. I was surprised to see Dad and Uncle Albert quietly standing at the gravesites with tears slowly dripping down their cheeks. They were very stoic and didn't say anything to each other or to me.

The car radio was turned off. All I heard was Uncle Albert complaining about his TV. He didn't like President Kennedy, and he missed all of his favorite TV programs like The Ed Sullivan Show because of all the news features about the assassination and funeral. Dad just rolled his eyes at me.

Although I hated to agree with the Grouch, it was true. Everywhere we looked, especially on TV, we saw commemorative souvenirs that celebrated Kennedy's life and presidency. Things like books about his life and death, framed photos, magazines, commemorative plates and statuary were promoted and sold everywhere. The November 29th "Life" magazine with Kennedy's photograph framed in a black border on the cover was especially prized. It was sold out everywhere. Dad couldn't find a copy even though we stopped at every open gas station along the way which wasn't many.

When we finally made it home, it felt weird being at our house for Thanksgiving. We always went to Grandma's, but so many cousins had moved Mom volunteered to host Thanksgiving at our home. At home, Uncle Albert complained because Mom wouldn't let him smoke his stinky cigar in the house. He kept it in his mouth unlit. Dad just rolled his eyes at Mom.

Thankfully, Larry had invited me to his house for their turkey dinner before our turkey dinner. I was starving and had never eaten two turkey dinners on Thanksgiving before today. I wondered if

I could handle them both as I jogged to Larry's happy to be away from Uncle Albert. After dinner, Larry was coming back to our house for our dinner. On my way to Larry's, I mostly thought about what I wanted for Christmas.

Larry's mom's Thanksgiving dinner menu was a lot like ours and guests always brought something for the table. They had a honey-colored roasted turkey on a platter that could've fed three families. The dining room table had a white tablecloth and a lit candelabrum. It was crammed with large bowls of dressing, mashed white potatoes and gravy, mashed sweet potatoes with toasted marshmallows, green beans mixed with mushroom soup and fried onion rings, homemade dinner rolls and real butter. His mom used her best silverware which Larry and his sisters hand polished.

Larry had an Uncle Albert too, but he was a pompous priest named Monsignor Payne. When the Monsignor, which is what he expected everyone to call him, said Grace before dinner, he said it first in Latin. Then, he repeated the prayer in English for the "little pagans." The Monsignor didn't call kids by our real names; he called us "pagans."

Since I didn't understand any Latin except Pig-Latin, after he finished the blessing, I looked him square in the eyes, smiled, and said in Pig-Latin, "Ankthay ouyay onsignormay!" [Thank you, Monsignor!] with a dash of smirk.

Quickly and smoothly, he smirked me back with a twinkle in his eye and a devilish smile. "Ebay arefulcay aganpay roay ou'llyay ogay otay ellhay." [Be careful pagan, or you'll go to hell.]

Larry and I sat wide-eyed and slack-jawed realizing the Monsignor knew Pig-Latin, and had bested my smirk. I didn't think anybody else at the table understood what had just happened until Larry's dad winked, as he passed the bowl full of sweet potatoes. "Oday ouyay antway weetsay otatoespay ickeymay?" [Do you want sweet potatoes, Mickey?]

Shaken to my core, all I could mutter was, "Yes, please." Everyone was smiling but Larry and me. We had always thought we had a secret language, and now we knew we didn't. What had we said over the years that the adults had heard? This wasn't good.

After everyone ate thick wedges of homemade apple pie because the Monsignor didn't like pumpkin pie, the kids cleaned the dinner table and took out the garbage. The women hand-washed the dishes as the men drifted off to the living room with a glass of Mogen David Concord wine. As soon as we got free from our chores, Larry and I trotted off to my house for our second Thanksgiving dinner.

As we trotted through St. Kevin's playground, we got the idea to check out the farm from last Sunday. It was only a mile or so out of our way. The whole way we yakked about the fun we were going to have over the holidays at the farm. We hadn't told anybody. The farm was our secret.

After we got to the top of the hill and ran past the barn, we were stupefied to see the smoldering black and gray skeleton of the old farmhouse. All that was recognizable was the three-story red brick fireplace and the front porch steps which were still attached to part of the wrap-around front porch. All f the cool banisters and the rest of the house were gone.

"What happened, Larry? We were here just a few days ago," and then I'm embarrassed to say I started crying. It was just a few tears nothing messy or blubbering.

The sadness of the moment hit me hard. The thought of all of those years of family memories burned up for no reason seemed tragic. Then it hit me. I had forgotten about the old trunk full of old family photos. "What happened to the treasure chest in the attic? It must've gotten burned up too, Larry."

"I don't know, Mickey. I didn't hear anything about a fire. Neither Mom or Dad mentioned one to me. I didn't see it on TV."

"I didn't either. I'll bet Booger and Butch started the fire though."

"Why would they do it? The house was so cool."

"Remember? Joey and the guys saw them start one here. We've got to tell, Joey," I said as I started to run home as fast as I could with Larry trying to keep up. About halfway down the rocky lane,

I saw a police car with its big red bubble gum mahcine lights on top coming up the hill. It was Officer Rogers. He stopped, got out and waved to stop me.

"Happy Thanksgiving, boys. It seems like you're always in the wrong place, Mickey. Didn't I see you at the Airway Drive-In hanging out in the back row the last time we saw each other? This is Thanksgiving. Why in God's name are you and Larry here trespassing instead of being at home? Do your parents know you're here?"

"No, sir," I said, shaking my head vigorously from side to side, and after stammering a few seconds, I told Officer Rogers most of the truth, which was easier than I thought. I also told him I thought Booger and Butch started the fire.

"Thanks for the tip, Mickey, but it wasn't those two hoods. It was a couple of hobos. They started a fire in the house to keep warm and a burning log must've rolled out of the fireplace. Evidently, they've been living here for quite a while and were stealing kids' bikes to sell them. Their names are Red and Jake. Have you seen any older, scraggly dressed men around the city lately, boys?"

"No, sir," I lied, as quickly as Larry said, "Sure you did, Mickey. Those guys must be the same guys you saw that night. Remember? You told me all about them." As Larry spoke, his voice got quieter and quieter. He remembered we saw those men when we snuck out of the clubhouse late at night last summer. I was stuck.

I had to defend myself because my friend just called me out in front of a police officer.

It's uncomfortable when you get caught in a lie. You feel like a pan of water the moment it boils over. It's the precise moment when your blood pressure has risen to the point your face turns cherry red, especially your neck and cheeks, from the embarrassment of being caught. All the while your face is turning unnatural shades of red your nose starts itching. It's the Pinocchio effect. You actually think your nose is growing longer because you lied. While trying to smile innocently, without scratching your nose to confirm it's growing, you look the other person directly in the eyes to prove you're telling the truth.

During your uncontrollable embarrassment, the person who is being lied to becomes conscious of your predicament. You know they suspect you're lying, and they return your smile with cunning and sometimes cruelty with relish.

Both you and they realize you're trapped unless you discover outer-earthly powers like a superhero. It's like a Tom and Jerry cartoon. Instead of going for the kill the cat just slaps the mouse around and watches it panic and run in circles. If you're the mouse, you'd rather be anywhere else unless you're the ever-clever Jerry.

Officer Roger's smile was benign but his penetrating eyes bored a hole into my soul. "When and where did you see these men? He didn't ask if I saw them, he asked where I saw them. He knew.

My nose itched like it was growing an inch per second. "Oh, yeah, oh, yeah," I said as I snapped my fingers and stuttered playing for time while I thought things through. "I think I remember what Larry's talking about Mister er' Officer Rogers. It was a long time ago. I'm not sure," I said as I stalled. I felt like Perry Mason. He was everyone's favorite TV attorney.

"Well Larry, why don't you tell me what you remember Mickey telling you. Maybe that will help him remember," demanded Officer Rogers as he cross-examined Larry.

Larry's face went from flesh-colored to pink to cherry red and finally to raspberry in three seconds. He looked like a mod color-changing chameleon. "Well, I'm not sure exactly, Officer Rogers. I think it was last summer. Wasn't it, Mickey?" Larry was looking at me for forgiveness more than reassurance.

"Yeah, I think it was Larry," I said, letting him slowly stew in his own juices. "Last summer, yeah, that's right. We were playing hide and seek that night and I saw a couple of raggedy men walking down the alley."

"Did you say anything to them?"

"No sir," I said, my lies coming easily. "I was sitting in a tree I climbed."

"Do you remember anything else, Mickey?"

"No, sir. It was dark, and we were playing hide and seek."

"Okay, thanks, now you boys better climb into my squad car. I'm going to take you home. I don't want you to get in any trouble on Thanksgiving."

"That's okay, Officer Rogers," I said, "We're just going to my house for dinner."

"Climb in boys," he said, pointing his finger to the back door of his car, "I want to make sure you get home on time." With dread, we silently climbed inside and he drove us home telling us not to return to the farm. He said it was dangerous, and besides, they were going to tear it all down next week. Shocked and sad, we asked him why. He told us they were going to build the largest shopping mall in the world there. "It's going to be called Northwest Plaza."

It seemed like everybody in the neighborhood was outside when Officer Roger's car pulled up in front of our house, and the three of us got out. Mom met us in the middle of the front yard.

"What did they do, Officer Rogers?"

Everybody was looking at Larry and me when he said with a wry smile, "Oh nothing, Mrs. McBride. I saw the boys walking along and I thought it would be a treat for them to get a ride in my squad car. Did you like it, boys?"

"Oh, it was great," said Larry, "but it wouldn't be as much fun if you were taking us to jail."

"That's an excellent thing to remember, Larry," said Officer Rogers. "What about you, Mickey? Do you want to come down to City Hall and see what the jail looks like?" he said with an in-your-face laugh.

"No, sir. Riding in the car was swell though, thanks."

"Where's Joey, Mrs. McBride? He and Mickey are usually together."

"He's home today. We don't know what's going on with him. His legs are so achy, he can hardly walk. I'm going to take him to the doctor. He walks like an old man."

"I'm sorry to hear that. Do you want me to take Joey to the hospital now?"

"No. No, thanks, we pray it's not that serious but Joey needs to be seen if he's not better soon. My mom's here. She's a nurse, and she's watching him."

"Okay but if you change your mind, just call the station. I can be here in a few minutes."

"Thanks, Officer. Can I get you some Thanksgiving food? I hate the thought of you not being home with your family today."

"No, Mrs. McBride. I don't want to put you through any trouble. I'm off tonight at seven."

"It's no problem at all. Mickey run inside and ask your Grandmother to cut a big piece of pie for Officer Rogers."

"No thanks, Mrs. McBride. I can't afford to buy new uniforms this year," he said as he chuckled and walked to his car, "Happy Thanksgiving, and you boys stay out of trouble. Do you hear me?"

"Yes, sir. Thank you, sir. Happy Thanksgiving, sir!" we sang in choir-like unison as we breathed a sigh of relief. It was almost dark outside.

Firing up her mother's intuition Mom said, "I know there's more to this than what Officer Rogers told me, boys, but I don't have time to talk about it now. Get inside and get cleaned up for dinner."

"Yes, Ma'am," we sang in perfect pitch and unison.

After we got in the house, Larry and I rushed to find Joey and tell him all of the news we had learned. I was stunned to see him still lying in bed dressed in his pajamas looking through Uncle Albert's View-Master with postcards spread out all over.

"Get out of bed, Joey. It's Thanksgiving," I urged. "Do you want to miss dinner?"

"Mind your own business, Mickey. I'm not feeling good. My legs hurt like crazy. It's tough to even walk across the room."

"You should go to the doctor's office then. This has been going on a long time, Joey."

"Mom's going to take me." Then we told Joey everything we had seen and learned from Officer Rogers. He asked lots of questions until we were finally called for dinner.

Eating a second Thanksgiving dinner was harder than I thought it would be. I was still full from Larry's family dinner because we didn't get to play at the farm like we wanted. Eating felt like forcing two pounds of something into a one-pound sack. I focused on eating my favorites which were the white turkey meat with salt and pepper, candied sweet potatoes with marshmallows and dressing with gravy. Joey barely ate. Mom was worried and kept telling him to eat more.

Uncle Albert put a damper on our fun. He sounded cross even when he was asking someone to pass the mashed potatoes and gravy. Fortunately, his sour disposition didn't affect Grandma even though she was sitting right next to him. Contrary to him, Grandma always sounded like she was smiling even when she asked you to pass the butter. I made sure to sit on her other side.

Throughout dinner Grandma teased and flattered Uncle Albert into a better mood. She complimented him on how dapper he looked, she told him how impressed she was with his View-Master collection, and she asked him about his travels to California. She even hinted she was going to Los Angeles next summer with a Cousin Louise. By the time Mom was ready to serve the pumpkin pie, Uncle Albert was smiling like he'd just found a silver dollar.

When he smiled, he still looked peculiar to me. I had never seen him smile before today.

Fortunately, he couldn't see well enough to see me gawk as I helped clean the table to serve the pumpkin pies.

I didn't believe people who said they didn't like pumpkin pie or desserts. What was wrong with them? Sugar was good. Who didn't love brownies, especially blonde brownies, and every cookie except a stale one? No sane person ever said, "Thanks, I don't want any ice cream on top of my birthday cake."

Desserts were royalty in my book, and Pumpkin Pie was the king with its own holiday. Some argued cakes got birthdays. They didn't. The birthday person always got to choose any dessert they wanted. You never knew what you were going to eat at someone's birthday party.

One time, I went to a birthday party and the kid wanted Saltine Crackers. What was he thinking? You can have Saltine Crackers any time. What a waste. Striped peppermint candy canes at Christmas didn't qualify as an authentic holiday dessert either. They were a tradition along with decorated cookies, fudge and a whole platter of snacks like chocolate-dipped pretzels. None of those were a full-fledged holiday dessert like pumpkin pie.

Another family tradition we have with our pumpkin pie was a princely squirt of "real" whipped cream propelled by nitrous oxide from the fluted spout on a red, white and blue can of Reddi-Wip, another of our favorite St. Louis products.

Mom said it was all about family traditions, "Traditions build families," and Mom had a tradition for every holiday. She made cherry pies for Washington's Birthday and gave us Tootsie Rolls as logs for Lincoln's. On Valentine's Day, we ate a red heart-shaped cake. On St. Patrick's Day, we dyed a tousle of our hair and wore green. On Memorial Day, July Fourth and Labor Day Mom made lemonade and we had a barbecue. Every summer, we went on a vacation. For our birthdays, Mom made each person whatever dessert they wanted, and she'd put the correct number of lit candles on it so we could sing happy birthday.

None of us suspected Uncle Albert was about to start a new Thanksgiving tradition. We were passing the can of Reddi-Wip around the table when Uncle Albert shook it and squiredt a dollop on his pie. His squirt defied all normal laws of physics and science. Somehow, he held the can at such an angle a hefty squirt of whipped cream deflected off the top of his pie onto Grandma's right cheek. Shocked, Grandma instantaneously jumped out of her kitchen chair and exclaimed, "Why you mischievous sprite. I had no idea you were such a good shot, Albert."

His squirt qualified as a Buffalo Bill circus shot and it caught all of us, especially Grandma, by surprise. Everyone, including Grandma, started belly laughing until tears ran down our cheeks.

Everybody that is except Uncle Albert. He didn't see what happened. So, he accused everyone of teasing him and he denied he had done it.

"It's impossible," he said. "I wouldn't do something like that to Ruth. You're just teasing me," he said indignantly. "Do I have food on my shirt or something?" he said feeling his shirtfront and tie.

He was wearing this guileless smile so none of us knew if he had done it on purpose.

"There's nothing on your tie Uncle Albert but you need some more whipped cream on your pie," teased Joey with a straight face. Promptly, Uncle Albert squirted and it happened again.

The dinner crowd went whacky. The odds against a blind man doing what he did, twice, were colossal. None of us had ever witnessed anything like it, and he did it twice precisely the same way in less than two minutes. He hadn't taken any wind calculations, measured the angle of deflection or the height of his target. The only difference between the two squirts was that on the second one he hit the collar of Grandma's dress before the splotch settled on her cheek. The "real" whipped cream, propelled only by nitrous oxide and perhaps cunning, traveled at the speed of a bullet and at such a trajectory it caromed off the slice of pie and hit Grandma squarely on the cheek two times.

Everyone at the table was laughing like hyenas. Uncle Albert sat there looking saintly with this innocent smile as if nothing had happened.

"What's so funny now?" asked the enigmatic Uncle Albert.

"They're acting crazy," said Joey, "but you still need some whipped cream."

Before Uncle Albert could press the fluted spout a third time, Grandma's hand shot out faster than a speeding bullet, snatched the can and shot Joey in the face. A new Thanksgiving tradition was born.

As the red, white and blue can of Reddi-Wip went around the table, theories abounded about how Uncle Albert had done it. Some shook the steel can an even number of times, others an odd number adding witchcraft to physics. Some used their right hand while others used their left to adjust the angle of the can. Dad rubbed his hands together vigorously so their warmth would heat the can to just the right temperature before launching the "real" cream. All he got for his efforts were small red hot spots on the palms of his hands. Nobody duplicated what Uncle Albert had blindly done, twice. Most of the serious researchers took a second piece of pumpkin pie to get a second shot, literally.

Since nobody else could do it, we all agreed it must've been blind luck. By the end of dinner, I still wasn't sure. Uncle Albert continued to claim it didn't happen but he smiled the rest of the night, and his smile got a little bigger each time someone told the story.

On our drive to take Uncle Albert home, he and Dad made small talk about the day, the times, and their lives. I couldn't relate to most of what they said about the "ol' days" and "kids today." I was lying across the backseat daydreaming about Christmas and trying to avoid the cloud of grey cigar smoke overhead until it escaped out of the side windows.

I fell asleep wondering if Uncle Albert had squirted Grandma on purpose. Once was probably an accident but twice meant he did it on purpose. Had I misjudged him all of these years? Perhaps it wouldn't be so bad if Uncle Albert came for Christmas.

☙

CHAPTER 8

CHRISTMAS TIME (IS HERE AGAIN)

Thanksgiving was entirely over. Anyone who put tinsel on a Christmas tree before putting away their pilgrim and turkey candles had their priorities wrong. They didn't seem grateful enough for having two such wonderful holidays within a month of each other. Besides, no one had gotten over Kennedy's assassination yet, and we needed as much joy as we could muster. Everyone was slowing their life down to pay extra attention and appreciate their family more. They relished opportunities to overcome the grief they felt for President Kennedy.

Christmas wasn't a one and done daylong holiday like the other twelve federal holidays in the year. It was a holiday that grew in excitement during the little bit left of November and most of December flew by in eager anticipation of eye-popping plates of hand-decorated cookies and a mound of colorfully wrapped gifts under the tree.

Kids got so anxious for Santa to come bouncing down their chimney, or in the case of our house the furnace vent, they couldn't sleep at night. Parents were always reminding their kids about Santa's list of naughty kids who got nothing but a lump of black coal in their stockings. Fortunately, I never got a lump of coal. I figured Santa's elves weren't very good spies.

Christmas traditions were a state of heart and mind. Throughout the entire month parents and teachers reminded us to be thoughtful and do kind things for other people. Being self-centered could result in a lump of coal. Christmas climaxed with the celebration of baby Jesus' birth in a Bethlehem stable. Truth be told kids were more excited about Santa Claus coming to town.

Christmas time was the best time of the year. Everyone started getting ready for Christmas months and even a year in advance especially if there were 75% off sales on Christmas cards and decorations on the Day After Christmas Sale at Famous-Barr and Stix Baer & Fuller stores.

Christmas time was the busiest time of the year. Nobody had enough time to decorate their home, write and address holiday cards, shop and wrap gifts. By Christmas Day, the emotional momentum built into a crescendo of celebration and crying kids. This was why someone very smart, maybe a rocket scientist or a department store Santa Claus about to have a nervous breakdown, invented Christmas Vacation. Everyone needed a short vacation to get over Christmas and rest up for New Year's Day, the first tradition of the New Year.

Christmas time at school meant the teachers, kids and room-mothers decorated classrooms, made gifts and went into the charity business. After school, kids transformed into shrewd merchants and professional fundraisers. They raised money for our various clubs, teams and troops by selling cases of candy and trinkets. Kids also collected money for the poor to earn religious statues and icons. During lunchtime, the student choir practiced three-part harmony for Midnight Mass. During classes, students wrote and rehearsed their school plays which would be produced and presented the last couple of days before Christmas Vacation.

Troop 643 of the Boy Scouts of America celebrated Christmas by selling boxes of Christmas candy to raise money for new tents and camping equipment. We also finished our Citizenship Project where we winterized poor people's homes in the city. We didn't plan camping or hiking trips during December. We were so darned busy doing things for others we didn't have any time for ourselves. I always put a couple of Boy Scout items on my Christmas gift wish list like a sleeping bag or something to carve. I got a hatchet to cut firewood last year.

Kids in the City of Saints dreamed about having a Christmas full of white fluffy snow so we could go sledding, make snow forts and have snowball fights but snow was rare. Usually, we were glowering at frozen brown grass mocking us as we looked to heaven for a white Christmas miracle.

Christmas time was off to a rare and unusual start when Dad took me for a hamburger, fries and a "root beer fishbowl" at the Chuck-A-Burger Drive-In Restaurant. We rarely ate out and when we did it wasn't a cool restaurant like Chuck-A-Burger. When we went to nice restaurants for rare events, we had to dress like we were going to church.

"This is great, Dad, thanks. What a way to start Christmas. It's too bad Joey and Mom aren't with us."

"Yeah, it's great to be here with you, Mickey," and then I saw it. There was a tear running down Dad's right cheek.

"What's the matter, Dad? Are you okay?"

"Yeah, I'm fine, Mickey. It's Joey."

"Joey? What's wrong with Joey, Dad? Where are Mom and Joey? Why aren't they here with us?"

"Joey's been admitted to Cardinal Glennon Children's Hospital. He's not coming home until they find out what's wrong with him. Mom is with him until he gets settled into his room."

I couldn't stand the thought of Joey being stuck in a hospital. Hospitals were for old, sick people. My own tears started flowing. How could my big brother be in the hospital? It seemed impossible.

"There's nothing wrong with Joey, Dad. His legs just ache a little. That's all. Let's go get him, Dad," I said as I stood and started wrapping my burger up in a napkin. By now, I was crying so hard I had to wipe my face on the sleeve of my jacket. "Let's leave, Dad," I pleaded.

"Sit down, Mickey. Finish your dinner. I thought you liked this place," he said calmingly as he wiped the tears from his eyes with his handkerchief.

"I do Dad but Joey is going to be scared. He needs us to be there with him, Dad. Let's go. Please? We can take the food with us."

"We can't go tonight, Mickey. Joey's going to be fine. Mom's with him. Sit down. You'll see. Let's eat our dinner and then go home. Okay?"

We sat and ate the rest of our dinner in silence. We each kept to our own thoughts. I wasn't sure what a dad thought about in these dark moments but I knew what a brother was thinking.

I was replaying our last moments together before I left for school. We were laughing when I hit Joey with a pillow because he was still lying in bed. I called him "Lazybones." Mom was going to take Joey to see Doctor Simon. It didn't seem like a big deal. I thought he'd get a shot or some pills and he'd come home. As hard as I tried not to, I kept thinking about our friend Allen who drowned last summer and about President Kennedy. I was sure Joey wouldn't die but I said a prayer anyway. How did he end up in the hospital? The thought of him in a hospital was more than I could bear to think about.

After we ate, we got up silently and started to leave. The cute waitress smiled at us and said, "Your brother's going to be fine. Don't worry. Do you hear?" We nodded our thanks.

I laid in bed, awake and waited for Mom to come home. It was late when I heard her and Dad talking in muffled tones. Mom was crying.

When Joey awoke in the middle of the night, he listened to all of the hushed hallway hospital sounds. Nurses were walking to the kids crying out in the night. It was unfamiliar and somewhat scary as he looked around his darkened room. He had never felt starched white sheets before. He was surprised to see a nurse dressed in her white cap and white uniform sitting in a straight back white metal chair next to the headboard of his white metal hospital bed.

Her eyes looked closed when she said, "Hello, Joey. You should be asleep. Aren't you tired?"

"Grandma? Is that you? You look like a real nurse."

"Well, that's because I am you silly cowboy. And tonight, I'm your private nurse. Do you need anything? Here take a sip of water."

"Thanks, Grandma. I'm nervous. What's going to happen? Why did Doctor Simon put me in the hospital? It's just my legs that hurt a little. I think I'm getting better."

"We're not sure why your legs hurt, Joey. That's why you're in the hospital. Doctor Simon is a good doctor. He'll figure out what's wrong."

"How long will I be here, Grandma?"

"Only as long as you need to be, Joey. Now, let's get some sleep. Tomorrow's a big day. You need your rest."

"Okay, Grandma. How's, Mickey? I'll bet he's worried. Can he visit me?"

"He's fine, Joey. He told me to tell you he's going to play with all of your toys until they break," she laughed. "I'm sorry but they don't let children visit patients. I'll give him any messages you want to send him though. Now, let's get some sleep."

"I love you, Grandma."

"I love you too, Joey more than you can know. Goodnight."

The sad news about Joey traveled faster than a Mercury space capsule. By the time I got to school, everyone at St. Kevin knew Joey was in the hospital. All of the kids in his class, especially the girls, were giving me messages to give him. His teacher sent him homework. Christmas time had taken another wrong turn but everyone seemed determined to get past it. The most frustrating part was I didn't know any more than anyone else. After two weeks of hospital tests, we still didn't know what was making Joey sick.

I felt guilty my life had actually gotten more exciting since Joey was admitted to the hospital. Grandma called me regularly to give me Joey's messages and updates. Mom and Dad went to the hospital every day, and most nights, so I stayed with our neighbors. The mothers felt horrible for me, so they made special dinners and desserts. Best yet, it was Christmas time. The mothers were always making cookies and fudge and sending the extras home for Joey and me.

One man bought a box of Boy Scout candy for me to give Joey. It took all of my Christmas spirit not to eat it. The harder I prayed for Joey, the more stuff I seemed to get, so, I prayed all the time for all kinds of stuff, including Joey. Miss Kann even suggested to my class they let me play Santa in our class play. My life was amazing. I was a celebrity. Even the older kids gave me attention when they asked about Joey.

I felt bad for Joey, but his misfortune was working out pretty good for me. It was when I'd get home and see his empty bed that I'd feel sad again.

All of the Christmas decorations and outside lights were up at our house except for our Christmas tree. Whenever I ran an errand to Kroger's, I'd hear Nat King Cole or Perry Como crooning Christmas carols and watch moms fill their shopping carts with flour, sugar, sprinkles and chocolate. Everyone felt the Christmastime spirit as they hummed along.

We hadn't gotten any snow yet but it didn't really matter if it fell during the week. Father Christiansen had declared he would never close school due to snow. He said when he had previously closed school for snow all of the kids were outside playing by eight in the morning. We were pretty sure all of the mothers had gotten him aside and threatened to stop volunteering if he ever closed school for snow or bad weather again. Most of the kids walked to school since we didn't have buses. Due to my luck with praying, I started praying for snow over our Christmas Vacation. It would be the best time for everyone and it seemed like the 'Christmassy' thing to do.

What we got instead was a frigid cold snap that froze all of the creeks, lagoons and ponds in and around St. Louis. Dad took me downtown to visit Santa and see all of the majestic decorations at the Famous-Barr and Stix Baer & Fuller stores. We drove onto the granite brick levy next to Eads Bridge first. It was an incredible sight.

We saw the Arch being built standing alongside the mighty Mississippi River which was churning monstrous muddy chunks of ice in the roiling frozen river. The Admiral was gone and I didn't see any rusty barges running up and down the river either. The Mississippi manhandled the massive chunks of ice as if they were toy blocks.

"I'm not sure I want to visit Santa today, Dad. I think I'm too old."

"Well, it's up to you, Mickey. You know if you don't believe in Santa, he's sure not going to give you any Christmas presents."

"I know but all I'd ask him for is to make Joey well and get him out of the hospital. Besides, it's not really Santa. It's only one of his helpers."

"Well, Mickey, I'm not sure that's Santa's job. That's above his pay grade. You should pray if you're asking about Joey. Dr. Simon told Mom this morning Joey's got rheumatic fever. It's a rare disease but it's not polio or cancer, thank God."

"Is that good or bad, Dad? Will Joey get well?"

"They don't really know much about rheumatic fever, Mickey. Your Mom is researching it. Joey's definitely going to be in the hospital a while longer. Our biggest fear is that he will get heart damage if he doesn't get totally well."

"Is Joey coming home for Christmas, Dad?"

"I'm not counting on it, Mickey. Let's just pray he gets well."

"I am, Dad. I'm praying all of the time. I really miss him. I haven't seen him for weeks," I sniffed through my frozen tears as Dad gave me a hug.

"Come on, Mickey. Let's go see the department stores' Christmas windows and Famous-Barr's Santa Land. The paper said they're better than they've ever been. You can decide later if you want to visit Santa."

We took a final look at the frozen Mississippi as it slammed titanic-sized chunks of ice against the Eads Bridge piles. Just the screeching sound of the ice scraping against the piers raised the hairs on the back of my neck.

Famous-Barr had dedicated an entire floor of its thirteen-floor department store to Santa Land. It was a fantastical sight to see dozens of decorated Christmas trees along a meandering path that featured dressed up elves and the latest Christmas gift sensations. After deciding it couldn't hurt, I visited Santa to ask him for a Beatles' album, a catcher's mitt and some socks and underwear.

I had a theory about Santa. Every year I got practical stuff for Christmas like socks, ties, belts, and underwear wrapped in

Christmas paper with bows. I never asked for any of them. It seemed like cheating when Santa mixed a bunch of stuff I had to wear to school and church with an Elliott Ness snub nose pistol stuffed in a black rubber shoulder holster. Oh well, what are you going to do? The big guy made all of the decisions. I figured I'd get "good-kid credit" by asking for socks and underwear to improve my odds for getting cool gifts I really wanted. It felt awkward sitting on Santa's lap. His beard looked too perfect and his bright red velvet suit looked way too big. Besides, he didn't have real black boots. They were just black vinyl spats that covered his black shoes.

Dad and I had never really spent much time together without Joey or Mom being with us. He grew up in the city and he knew where to have fun. On our way home, we stopped at an A&W on Kingshighway to eat lunch. At lunch, Dad told me he had a surprise for us. After about 20 guesses, we drove our big-finned white Plymouth Fury I to Forest Park.

"We aren't going to the museum, are we?" I asked, begging him to say no.

"The museum? Are you kidding? Do I look like your teacher or your Dad, Mickey?" He smiled and winked as he drove to the lagoon at the bottom of Art Hill. The scene looked like one of the blue and white Currier & Ives dinner plates Mom collected from Kroger's grocery for .25 cents each a few years ago. We only used her dinnerware for major holidays like Easter, Thanksgiving and Christmas. She collected eight place settings and various serving pieces by buying a couple each week. The dishes were Mom's pride and joy and it took her a whole year to collect the entire set.

The Grand Basin lagoon was crowded with ice skaters. Kids were playing tag and there was a long line of people doing a whip out in the middle of the lagoon. Everyone was laughing out loud and having a lot of fun.

"Shoot, Dad, we should've brought our ice skates," I said, sad we hadn't thought about ice skating before we left the house.

"Maybe you didn't think of them but I sure did," laughed Dad as he jumped out of the Plymouth and opened the trunk to get our skates.

We walked over to a roaring log fire on the edge of the lagoon. A bunch of people were standing and sitting around the fire because it was putting off a lot of heat, and it was cold. We found a couple of empty tree stumps to sit down and put on our skates careful to lace them tightly. At the top of Art Hill, we saw the Art Museum and the gigantic bronze statue of King St. Louis IX sitting astride his charger.

In a matter of minutes under a bright blue sky with large cottony white clouds, Dad was leading us through a channel of lagoons under decorative iron and concrete bridges that carried us throughout Forest Park. Ice skating had never been as much fun.

Our family had ice skated at Steinberg Ice Skating Rink before. It was especially fun at night but all we did was skate in huge counter-clockwise circles listening to Doris Day sing "How Much Is That Doggie in the Window?'" and "Que Sera Sera."

Joey and I tried to skate on Cold Water Creek a couple of times. The creek was too narrow and we had to step, or jump, over tree limbs and rocks all along the way. I had never skated as fast as I could go without someone, or something, making me stop or slow down. Today, it felt like I was flying over the ice. The lagoon's ice was as clear and as smooth as glass. I was skating as fast as I could to play tag and follow-the-leader with Dad and some kids we picked up as we raced around the lagoons. We went so fast the water in our eyes was freezing. I completely forgot about Joey which always kept me half sad. It felt great skating with Dad, and I decided I'd never forget this day for the rest of my life.

When we'd get cold, we'd stop at one of the fires on shore to get warm. One family gave us hot chocolate when we were headed back to find our shoes along the shoreline.

It was during that stretch of the lagoon that I learned the importance of a "saying." Older people like parents, grandparents and teachers always had sayings for everything whether they were "Happy as a songbird" or "Mad as a hornet." Adult men rarely cussed in public and only greasers, punks and tough kids cussed in front of kids or women. Adults used sayings or proverbs to colorfully express what they meant or how they felt. If you had a question or some other state of quandary and mentioned it to them, they'd recite a truism they'd heard in life. If none of their apothegms fit the moment, they'd make one up. Here are a couple of examples.

"Hey Mom, can I have a quarter to go to the movies this afternoon?"

"Mickey, you should know by now a penny saved is a penny earned. Use your soda bottle money."

Mom would ask, "Dad, do you really think you should drink another beer?"

And Dad would reply, "Mother, beer is proof God loves us and loves to see us happy."

In Indiana last summer, Uncle Willard had a colorful axiom for everything. He used sayings like, "He has a neck as long as a well rope," and, "She's so skinny, she can take a bath in a gun barrel." When he talked about politicians he said, "He's so crooked, he would steal pennies off a dead man's eyes," and, "He's got a mouth full of givemes." His maxims created pictures that made us laugh, I used one of his brocards all of the time now.

When someone said something mean and then acted like they were kidding I'd say, "You're as funny as a screen door on a submarine." Sayings were thoughtful and colorful; they made words come alive.

Grandma liked to get things done. She stayed busy. She'd say, "The early bird gets the worm, Mickey," and "A job worth doing is worth doing right." She never let a chance for a chore go undone because, "A stitch in time, saves nine."

Aphorisms were more than a clever turn of a phrase; they were instant wisdom.

Mom and Dad loved sayings so much they bought wallpaper for our kitchen that had morals printed all over it in green and red. I figured they referred to the wallpaper when we did something wrong or asked them a question.

A saw that became important to me today was, "You're skating on thin ice, Mister!" Mom and Dad used it to warn us for being disrespectful or misbehaving. They used it as a warning.

As Dad and I were flying along with the wind at our back, we saw a grandpa-looking man off in the distance take a hard fall onto the ice. After he fell, he laid there writhing in pain. Everyone at that end of the lagoon heard the thwack of him landing hard on the ice and his screams of anguish. Then, everyone did exactly what you'd expect. They skated over to see what happened and if he was hurt. In a minute or so, there were a hundred people or more surrounding the distraught man struggling on the ice.

One of the nearby onlookers said, "What's going on, Frank? I can't see. Is the old man alright?"

"I don't know. The old man fell hard on the ice, Margaret. He must've broken his leg or something by the way he's screaming."

"Is he with his family?"

"Not sure. Some of the men are trying to pick him up so they can carry him off the ice but he's in agony. I hope someone calls an ambulance. He must be hurt badly."

Then everybody heard it. At first, it was a subtle hissing sound. In seconds, the hissing became crackling sounds. Everyone watched as the sounds became visible cracks that raced lightning-fast all over the ice like a spider's web at the end of the lagoon. One fracture was about three inches deep in the ice, and it shot right between my skates.

In a fraction of a moment, everyone that gathered to help or rubberneck was racing away from the old man as fast as they could skate. They were afraid of falling through the ice. Even the four men that picked the old man up dropped him back on the ice and raced away the moment they saw the cracks beneath them. The old man was howling and writhing on the ice even louder now.

Skating on creeks and ponds we all heard horrible stories about people, especially younger kids, drowning. When the ice was too thin, it broke. I was never really sure the stories were true. I figured they were just trying to scare me so I'd be careful. In the future, I decided to listen more carefully when they told me one of their "sayings."

Faster than they had gathered to see what happened; the mass of people deserted the old man. He was left lying there all alone screaming in agony as a puddle of lagoon water rose around him and the surrounding ice continued to crack. The only person skating towards the old man was Dad.

"Stay back, Mickey. Go over to the fire on the shore."

"Wait. Don't go, Dad. It's too dangerous," I yelled frantically.

"Do what I say, Mickey," he sternly shouted over his shoulder as he raced away.

I didn't wait or question Dad, as he carefully skated and picked his way over to the old man while trying to soothe and settle him.

I skated to the shore and watched, Dad. I was afraid something would happen to him. Everyone watched breathlessly but nobody went to help. When Dad reached the old man, they were both in the growing puddle. Dad quickly grabbed the old man by the shoulders of his long woolen coat and slowly dragged him along the ice while he skated backwards to the shore. The man was screaming even louder.

As Dad got the man near the shore, two police officers came out on the ice to help. You could hear an ambulance's siren in the distance as everyone clapped and whistled for the old man and Dad. Dad was a hero. At that moment, I was as proud as I could be that he was my dad. Everybody went up to Dad, clapped him on his back and shook his hand.

"You're a hero, sir," said one of the police officers.

"Not me," said Dad, "Anybody could've done what I did."

"Yeah but nobody did. That's why you're the hero," he smiled.

Dad wasn't a comic book superhero like Superman, Batman or even Spiderman. He was a real-life hero. A living, breathing hero who helped an everyday person that needed help.

"You're a hero, Dad," I shouted as I ran up to hug him.

"No, I'm not, Mickey. I just helped a man that was hurt and needed help; that's all I did."

"But the ice was cracking, Dad. It was dangerous to be out on the ice. Everybody else skated away."

"Thank goodness they did too Mickey or the ice would've broken through and a lot of people could've gotten hurt. Maybe drowned."

"Everybody else was too afraid to do anything, Dad."

"I was afraid too Mickey, and I thought about it very carefully as I did it. I didn't want to just charge out there and cause a bigger problem."

When our feet were warm and dry and our shoes were on our feet, I realized our adventure was over. People were still coming up to Dad and telling him he was a hero.

"Thanks, Dad. I've never had more fun or been prouder."

"Me too, Mickey. We'll come down to Forest Park when it snows and go sleigh riding down Art Hill."

"That'd be so cool, Dad," and before I could say "faster than a shooting star," I was fast asleep on the Plymouth's blue vinyl seats. We were on our way home. I didn't wake up until Dad shook me at the Fina gas station's Christmas tree lot. Fathers and sons of another Boy Scout troop ran it.

"Come on, Mickey. Let's pick out our Christmas tree. It's time to put it up." Groggily, I climbed out, wiped the sleep from my eyes and followed Dad.

Christmas had lots of great smells. Many were delicious but nothing smelled more like Christmas than pine tar at a Christmas tree lot. Well, maybe chocolate chip cookies baking in the oven. Christmas tree shopping was another of our family traditions. It had fanfare, considerable discussion and negotiation. It ended with a cup of hot chocolate at home.

"What about Mom and Joey? What if we pick a tree they don't like?"

"Well then, they don't have to look at it, Mickey." He smiled as he walked towards the tree lot whistling "Silent Night." I was getting the feeling Dad was enjoying not having to answer to Mom for every decision he made.

"I'm right behind you, Dad."

"How about this one?" I asked, quickly pulling out a sparse looking five-foot Balsam Fir like we always decorated. "How does this one look?"

"It's nice but I'm thinking about buying something a little different this year. You know. Shake it up a little. Get a tree with some pizazz!" he said as he whistled over to another group of trees leaning on a wooden frame. I had never seen Dad like this.

Seeing and smelling the green cut trees leaned against the wooden frame reminded me of last year when Dave and I went to the Kroger tree lot. We spent all day hiding in the frames behind the trees. Silently, we spied on families shopping for their trees. The trees hid us. Most families laughed and had a good time. Others argued about which tree was taller or which was more beautiful and had fewer bare spots. A few kids argued saying they deserved to choose the tree this year because someone else decided last year. We could always tell who didn't get their way because they'd storm away and slam the car door.

As families scrutinized the trees and pulled them away from the frames, Dave and I would throw our voices like ventriloquists. We talked like we were the trees. We said things like, "Take me, take me. He's not very good looking. Look at his bare spots." or "Don't take him. Take me. My needles are going to last a lot longer."

Most of the people laughed and thought we were funny. Some people even talked to us and asked us questions. One guy asked us how much water we drank. Dave told him the tree only drank whiskey. The man laughed hard and bought the tree. We got caught when a little girl told an employee she heard a tree talking to her parents. He was a Grinch and didn't have much of a sense of humor. He chased us away but we went back later.

"If you want something different, Dad, why don't we get a cool silver aluminum tree? They have a spinning wheel that slowly changes the color of the aluminum tree from red to blue to green. Remember, we saw one at the hardware store?" I said, smiling and shaking my head up and down like a jack-in-the-box.

"I'm not sure we want something that different, Mickey. Do they come with sunglasses?" he laughed.

"Nope but we can get one where the aluminum tree spins in circles and plays Christmas music, Dad."

"We need a real Christmas tree, Mickey. One that smells like the outdoors. One where we can hang a string of colored lights and all of the family's ornaments with silver tinsel."

"Yeah, but we'd be the only family in the neighborhood with a silver aluminum tree. That'd be cool."

"Yeah but it might be too different for Mom. She likes Christmas traditions too much for a modern-looking aluminum tree. How about this Scotch Pine? I've always wanted a Scotch Pine tree."

"If you always wanted a Scotch Pine tree why didn't you just buy one?"

"It's not always about you or me when a person has a family, Mickey. It's about the family and finding what the family likes—together."

"Oh. Do we all like Scotch Pine trees, Dad?"

"Well, I do and I think Joey would. Don't you like them, Mickey?"

"They're okay, Dad, but I really like aluminum trees, and I think Joey would like one too. What about Mom? Does Mom like Scotch Pines?"

"Not really, she thinks they're too hard to hang ornaments. I think the ornaments would look just fine though."

"Yeah, but it's not just about you, Dad."

Dad groaned as he pulled out a Balsam Fir and said, "How does this one look, Mickey? Is it full?"

"It looks pretty full to me but what about your Scotch Pine tree, Dad?"

"Oh, maybe next year, Mickey. We have enough going on this year without arguing about what kind of tree we got."

In a matter of minutes, Dad paid the two and a half dollars for the tree, tied it on top of the Plymouth, and we were driving down the Rock Road to go home.

By the time we got the Balsam Fir set in its stand at home, I was exhausted. I had never spent as much time with Dad as I had the past couple of weeks. Today had been especially magical. Usually, when Dad and I spent time together, we were doing chores like cutting the grass, tuning the car or raking the leaves. Occasionally, we played catch but he left for work before any of us woke up. After dinner, we did homework until we watched a little TV and then we'd go to bed by 9:30 p.m. The last couple of weeks he and I were together as much as Mom and I were usually together.

As I went to bed, I felt more relaxed than I had since Joey went to the hospital. I prayed he'd get home for Christmas. He was my big brother, and we had always gotten along well until the Jamboree.

ɛʋ

LADY MADONNA

"What do you mean, Mom?" asked Joey looking hopefully into her eyes.

"I mean you're going to get completely well, and you're going to get to come home for Christmas, Joey. That's what I mean," she said with a radiant smile on her face.

"How do you know? Did the doctor tell you? I've asked, and asked Dr. Simon a million times. He just keeps saying, 'We'll have to wait and see, Joey. Don't get your hopes up. Christmas in the hospital isn't so bad.' How are you so sure?"

"I just know, Joey," she said winking and nodding her head knowingly.

"Tell me how you know, Mom, please."

"I will if you promise not to laugh at me, Joey, and you can't tell anybody else."

"Not even Grandma?"

"Well okay, I've already told her and Dad but nobody else. Promise?"

"Okay, I promise."

"Mary told me."

"Mary? Mary who? Billy's mom?"

"No, silly. How would Billy's mom know? Jesus' mom, Mary. She told me," Mom said emphatically.

"Who?" said Joey shaking his head in disbelief and looking at her a little worried. Mom had been coming to the hospital every day for almost a month. She sat next to his hospital bed all day, and she followed him throughout the hospital for his tests. They even cried together after he'd gotten his bone marrow test. It was very painful.

"When did you see Jesus's mom?" he asked worriedly.

"Mary told me last night, Joey."

"Mary talked to you last night?"

"Not exactly talked, Joey. She smiled at me."

"What are you talking about, Mom?" asked Joey. He was starting to get really worried about his mom. Maybe the strain was too much for her, he thought.

"Well, last night I went to Devotions at church, like I do every Thursday night. After Devotions I stayed, and I prayed my Novena directly in front of Mary's statue. After my prayers, I asked Mary to please help you get well and to let you get home for Christmas. Then, Mary smiled right at me."

"She smiled at you, Mom?"

"Yes, it was such a beautiful sweet smile. I've never seen such a loving, peaceful and knowing smile before, Joey. It was a miracle. The statue of Mary smiled right at me. At first, I couldn't believe what I was seeing. Mary looked me in the eyes and smiled at me straight into my heart."

"Did anyone else see her smile, Mom?"

"No one else was in church at that time. It was after Devotions. It was just the Blessed Mother and me."

"Well, what did you do or say, Mom?"

"I couldn't say anything. I was dumbstruck. At first, I didn't believe my own eyes but the Blessed Mother just continued to smile and look right at me. Reassuring me. So, I just looked at her and smiled. That's all I could do, Joey. I just smiled back, and I knew what she was telling me."

"What happened then?"

"Then, in an instant, Mary's glorious smile was gone, and I was looking at the stone face of the statue again. Mary's sublime smile just vanished."

"How are you sure you saw her, Mom? How do you know what Mary meant?"

"I just know, Joey. I've been praying to Mary my whole life. I've asked her for help and prayed to say thanks for things she's done for us. I know Mary smiled at me last night. I believe she was telling me you're getting completely well, and you'll be home for Christmas. I believe Mary, and you have to believe her too, Joey."

"Okay, Mom, I promise. I believe. When I get well and get home for Christmas, will you give me something I really want?"

"Sure, Joey. Anything. What do you want for Christmas?" Mom was relieved Joey believed her.

"I want Streak and Mickey to pick me up in Streak's Nomad and drive me home from the hospital, Mom."

Mom looked stunned. Streak was the city's hotrod driving hellion every kid, and some dads, wanted to emulate.

"Well, I don't know if I can promise that, Joey. I can't make a promise that depends on somebody else. I'm not sure his car is safe. What if he won't do it?"

"He'll do it, Mom. He told me he'd do it when he visited me."

"Streak came to the hospital? When?"

"When he brought me that cool model hot rod I put together over there."

"Streak brought you that model? I thought Grandma brought it."

"No, it was Streak. He visited me late one night and brought me that model. He told me he'd bring me home in the Nomad when I got well. If you ask, Streak, he'll do it. I know he will." Joey was excited at the thought of riding home in Streak's neon yellow 1956 Nomad.

"Okay, I'll ask Streak, Joey but you have to believe Mary smiled and get well first."

"I believe, Mom."

❧

ACT NATURALLY

No place south of the North Pole compared to the noise and excitement created by kids in a grade school the week before Christmas. Each classroom was decorated with Christmas trees, ornaments, nativity scenes, holly leaves, berries and anything that could be cut and glued from colored construction paper. Adding to the festivities, the girls wore red and green ribbons and small bells in their hair that matched their uniforms. The boys were too cool for red and green decorations. We acted like we weren't excited and nothing unusual was happening but inside we were ready to explode like a champagne bottle.

Every teacher had two homeroom mothers who helped host a class Christmas party. The parties were complete with snacks, games and a class play. The classes' plays were theatrical performances and other classes were invited to watch. Not much book learning happened during the days before Christmas break. By the last day, the noise and excitement grew to such a Christmas crescendo Sister Mary George usually let us out of school early. Even her chrome whistle wasn't loud enough to drown out everyone to get us quiet.

Miss Kann had our class rehearsing our "Twas The Night Before Christmas" play for two weeks. Everyone had to practice their roles, gather props and make their costume for our off-Broadway production. Dad and I spent a week putting together my Santa costume. He also helped the boys in my class use cardboard boxes to build a fireplace. We painted it red to make it look like it was built from bricks. Santa needed a chimney.

We were a dedicated theatre troupe that rehearsed every day before and after school. None of us wanted to let Miss Kann down. We worked as hard as we could and did what she asked. The other classes were producing religious plays. The boys in those classes looked bored wearing shepherd and sheep costumes.

Today, we were excited to put on our premiere performance. Dressed in our costumes, we peeked out of our coatroom to watch four classes of first and second graders file into our classroom and take their seats. We brought in wooden benches for them to sit and moved our desks into the hallway.

JoAnne was selected to be our narrator. She got to read, "Twas the Night Before Christmas" because she was the best actress in our class. Miss Kann said JoAnne sounded dramatic and spoke with emotion. None of the boys cared we weren't chosen. We liked looking at JoAnne.

The stage was set. The fireplace was set up next to the coatroom, so I could go down and up the chimney easily. Dad helped decorate our real Scotch Pine Christmas tree with colored lights. We made a cardboard bed for 'Mama in her kerchief,' and a separate bed for 'Poppa in his nightcap.' Sister George said there was no way a boy and girl were going to be laying in or on anything remotely like a bed at St. Kevin while she was principal.

We turned off the overhead class lights and pulled down the window shades. We made a set of cardboard shutters so Poppa could open the shutters and throw up the sash. A couple of the guys used large Boy Scout flashlights as spotlights for the actors.

In the coatroom, I was sweating like a sinner in church. It felt like it was one-hundred and fifty degrees. I was wearing a red woolen stocking cap, a beard made from cotton balls, and a pillow belted over my stomach under Miss Kann's bright red winter coat. My only salvation was I smelled her perfume on the collar of her coat. I had red rouge on my cheeks and nose but I drew the line when the girls wanted to put light red lipstick on my lips. Miss Kann relented when the guys wouldn't stop razzing me.

It was so quiet you could've heard a partridge in a pear tree poop when the spotlight focused on JoAnne for her big moment. She planned to be a movie actress in Hollywood, and we planned to go to her movies. She dramatically promenaded to the center of our classroom, and started her narration. She had gotten Sister's special dispensation not to wear her uniform for her performances. She was dressed in her best Sunday dress and had curled Christmas ribbons pinned in her hair.

JoAnne started our play by telling the story about how and why Clement Clarke Moore had written his poem. The first and second-grade children, who most certainly believed in Santa, were enthralled with the lilt of her voice and her hand gestures. JoAnne seemed to have a slight yet dramatic English accent. After her introduction, she began the poem with a dramatic flair while Poppa [played by Kurt] snored just loud enough to be heard.

"Twas the night before Christmas [dramatic pauses and dramatic sweeping hands gesturing], and all thro' the house [more dramatic pauses and more dramatic sweeping hand gestures], Not a creature was stirring [finger to her lips], not even a mouse."

As JoAnne dramatically turned toward the chimney to showcase our fireplace and stockings with a sweeping hand gesture, one of the little kids whispered, "What's that?" just loud enough so everyone heard.

Undaunted, JoAnne persisted with more dramatic gestures and pauses, and an all-knowing tip of her chin and slight shake of her head, "The stockings were hung by the chimney with care; In hopes that St. Nicholas soon would be there."

Then in a not so quiet whisper one of the innocents, probably a first grader intent on going to hell, said in a very excited and shrill voice with more drama than even poor JoAnne could muster, "Is that a mouse that ran across her foot? It's coming over here. Help!" Then she stood, pointed to the floor and screeched even louder.

Soon shrill screeching screams, some of which were thankfully dog-whistle loud, replaced JoAnne's carefully crafted dramatic narration. Our play was interrupted and shut down as the young hellions jumped up and stomped their feet on the long wooden benches. The second graders pushed the weaker first graders back to the floor where they continued to jump up and down, shrieking, "Mouse, mouse, save me from the mouse." It was bedlam.

The darkened room added to the chaos as the guys with the spotlights focused their lights on their feet to keep the would-be marauding mouse from climbing up their legs. Even Kurt stood on his cardboard bed in his striped nightshirt and cap and shrieked like a first grader.

Distraught, JoAnne was beside herself as she stood in the middle of the classroom crying. She wasn't sure if she was crying about her broken performance or because she was afraid of the mouse. The chaos in our classroom was ruining our performance.

I wasn't sure if there was a mouse or not. I felt pretty safe standing on a chair in the coatroom sweating. The teachers weren't able to get the kids, who were now running in circles waving their hands like a Halleluiah Choir, under control. Resigned and somewhat relieved, I took off my costume to cool off and dry my face. This smeared my rosy cheeks and cherry nose. I looked more like a bleeding zombie at Halloween than a Santa at Christmas. We were a ball of confusion and chaos.

After the classroom was cleared of screaming and ungrateful kids, our faithful janitor Mr. Stewart dutifully hunted the marauding mouse in every nook and cranny of the classroom. He didn't find so much as a mouse hair. The little kid must've been hallucinating on gingerbread.

After lunch, we redeemed ourselves. We put our play on for a group of third and fourth graders that went perfectly. Everyone laughed and clapped, and JoAnne was the star. I lost about five pounds sweating but I made up for it by eating the candy canes we were going to give the little kids. Dad offered to pay to have Miss Kann's coat dry cleaned but she just laughed and thought nothing of it.

∽

CHAPTER 11

HAPPY XMAS (WAR IS OVER)

Mom told everyone it was a Christmas Miracle. Miraculously, Joey got well in a matter of days. There weren't any signs of lingering symptoms to his heart or anywhere else from his rheumatic fever. He was walking normally without any pain, so Dr. Simon released him to go home on the morning of Christmas Eve. It was just in time for the St. Ann Christmas parade.

Our family had our own parade assembled in front of Cardinal Glennon Hospital. We were waiting for Joey to be wheeled out and released. Grandma was in the lead car driving her Old Grey Mare. Dad's Plymouth was the last car. Streak's Nomad was trapped in between. A nun with a starched white habit that had a veil the size of a Big Boy's menu pushed Joey outside. He was sitting in a wooden wheelchair with wheels taller than my bike's. The nun looked flabbergasted, as she helped Joey into the black leather rolled and pleated front seat of the neon yellow Nomad.

Streak had his right hand on the chrome skull shifter knob. I was in the back seat with Streak's girlfriend and a grin as wide as the windshield. We wanted to be back in St. Ann by noon for the Christmas parade. Santa was landing in a helicopter.

As Grandma slowly pulled out onto Grand Boulevard for the drive home, Streak stomped on the gas pedal, laid some rubber, pulled around Grandma and shot down Grand Blvd. daring anyone to chase him.

The G-force of his 700-horsepower engine pushed us deep into the back of our seats. My head was pressed so deeply into the seat, I smelled the leather. "I can't drive behind your little Ol' Granny the whole way, guys. The Nomad will fall asleep," laughed Streak as he shifted into third gear.

I had a pretty good idea what Grandma, Mom and Dad were thinking and saying as Streak laid rubber with every shift. All we were doing in the Nomad was laughing, in my case nervously. We yelled over the reverberations of the howling Nomad as it sped its way to St. Ann. Everyone was left in our dust. When I looked back, Dad was racing to catch up with us to no avail.

We sped down the two-lane Rock Road to downtown St. Ann. Each wooden electric pole had a large plastic Christmas decoration attached to the top of it. Some decorations looked like yellow bells, some were giant green wreaths and others were red candles with yellow flames. Streak drove up to the barricades that were blocking the entrance of the Four Screen Drive-In where they were organizing and starting the parade. Streak honked his high-pitched awooga horn. My heart galloped when I saw Officer Rogers walk out. The last time I saw Streak and Officer Rogers together was at the Airway Drive-In last summer. It had been a showdown. I was surprised to see Officer Rogers smile at us and pull back one of the barricades to let us in the Drive-In entrance. He walked over to Joey's window.

"Merry Christmas, Joey! We're glad you got out of the hospital. We want you to be in the parade this year. You can ride in Streak's Nomad."

"Gosh thanks, Officer Rogers. Are you sure?"

"Absolutely. Streak called me and wanted you to be in the parade. So, we reached an agreement. Didn't we Streak?" He smiled at Streak and tipped his cap to Streak's girlfriend.

"Oh, hello Mickey. I didn't know you were here. You'll have to come with me to jail," he joked as I tried to think of what I had done.

"Enjoy the parade boys, and tell your folks Merry Christmas!"

"Yes, sir. Merry Christmas, sir!"

As the Nomad rumbled into the parade set-up area everybody's heads, including our friends from Troop 643, swiveled to look.

When the guys saw Joey in the front seat, they ran up to say hello and see how he was doing.

When my friends saw me sitting in the back seat with Streak's girlfriend, they ran up to my window to act like they wanted to say hello. They really wanted to look at her. Most of them couldn't even say my name without stuttering as they ogled her. When she put her arm over my shoulders and kissed me on the cheek, she told them she was my girlfriend. They acted goofy, Streak acted jealous, and I started stuttering.

"I didn't do anything, Streak, I promise," I said as I fumbled for an answer. "I guess she just likes me." We felt like celebrities.

Rumbling down the center of the Rock Road, the parade spectators went wild whenever Streak gunned the engine to spit fire out the carburetor and squeal the Nomad's tires. Inside the Nomad, it was so loud, we couldn't hear the Pattonville or Ritenour High School marching bands in front and behind us.

After the parade, which was too short, Joey and I climbed out of the Nomad in Kroger's parking lot.

"Thanks, Streak! I didn't have any idea how cool it would be to ride in the Nomad. I'll never forget the look on Grandma's face as we raced past her," smiled Joey.

"No problem, punk. It was a gas hanging out with you and the twerp," he said, pointing at me.

"I mean it, Streak. Coming to see me in the hospital, driving me home and getting us in the parade are things I'll never forget. Thanks!"

"Aww, don't get sappy, Joey. You're a good kid, and so is the twerp. Now, get out of here."

"Merry Christmas, Streak!"

"Merry Christmas, boys! Hang loose," and they peeled off in his Nomad.

It was a relief to watch Joey walk normally again as we watched the helicopter set down in front of Rexall's with our friends. Santa jumped out to raucous cheers of the Pattonville and Ritenour cheerleaders. Santa had a sack full of candy he threw to the crowd until it was gone. As I sucked on my peppermint candy cane, I hatched my plan to catch Santa, or Dad and Mom, that very night.

I had a burglarious nature when it came to uncovering the Christmas gifts Mom and Dad stashed throughout our house long before we opened them. Over the years, Joey and I had discovered all of their hiding spots. The secret closet under our basement steps was their favorite spot. To prove Santa wasn't real, I had to find one of his gifts before Christmas. Unfortunately, I didn't recognize Santa's handwriting on the gift tags as Grandma's, Mom's or Dad's handwriting.

Since my friends didn't believe in Santa anymore, I redoubled my efforts to find the hiding spots for Santa's gifts to prove he wasn't real. I even looked all through Grandma's house. Nothing. Nada. Zilch. I never found even a hint of Santa's gifts anywhere. Not even the trunk of the car had a gift. I couldn't find Santa's wrapping paper either. Every kid wanted to believe in Santa but maybe it was time to stop. I took a lot of grief. My parents told me I wouldn't get any gifts from Santa if I didn't believe in him. I wanted to believe in Santa but it was harder and harder to do it.

Dad stroked his chin and called it my 'Christmas conundrum.' I was stroking my chin when I told my parents I wanted to sleep in the family room of our new rathskeller by the Christmas tree tonight to catch Santa. They said they understood, agreed and wished me luck. They knew I couldn't stay up all night watching TV because it went off the air at midnight. I asked Joey if he wanted to stay up with me. He said he wanted to sleep in his own bed since it was the first time since Thanksgiving.

I yawned as I fidgeted with the family Kodak Instamatic camera. It was loaded with a flashbulb in case I got a chance to take Santa's photo. I was lying on the couch, staring at the colored lights strung throughout the tree. Lit Christmas trees with silver tinsel always looked their best in an otherwise completely dark room. I was captivated by a string of lights that looked like small colored candles that had liquid bubbling in them. Who invented those lights? Bored, I struggled unsuccessfully not to eat the Swiss cheese I had set out for Santa on one of Mom's Currier and Ives plates. In past years, we always set out chocolate chip cookies. This year, the Santa downtown told me, "Never underestimate the power of cheese, Mickey." Swiss cheese was my favorite, and I hoped it was Santa's too.

Last year to get the full dramatic effect of dozens of wrapped presents piled high under our lit Christmas tree, Mom and Dad waited until after Joey and I went to bed to put out our gifts. Not this year. They set out all of the family's gifts because they said they weren't going to stay up later than me. Everyone kissed me goodnight and went to bed. Grandma even tried to talk me into going to bed in my own room. I was steadfast. She just smiled.

"Okay. I hope Santa still stops, Mickey."

"He will, Grandma. If there really is a Santa," I smiled and winked smugly.

She seemed worried when she went to bed. Was I overplaying my hand with Santa? Maybe he quit going to my friends' houses when they stopped believing. Figuring it meant more gifts, I wanted to believe but I felt pressure from my friends. It was a conundrum for sure.

In case Santa was real, I spent time in thoughtful kid reflection. Kid reflection meant my mind skipped from Santa to Scouts to Santa to baseball to Santa to music to Santa to anything else after which I forgot about Santa. Switching my thinking about every two seconds. I wondered whether I'd been naughty or nice this year. After thinking about everything I could remember to think about, I figured I had been at least as good as last year or the years before. I wasn't perfect but I was as good as I could be. That's saying something, isn't it? Anybody can be a lot less well-behaved than they can be. Who's perfect besides God? Who is closer to being perfect than me? Well, probably a lot of people are. Grandma or a nun are for sure and perhaps Mom and Dad and a priest are too but the majority of guys I know aren't. For the most part, we try to do our best even when we don't, and we keep trying even when we haven't. I figured if Santa was real and he was giving everybody else gifts for not being perfect, I stood a pretty good chance of getting something this year too. If I believed.

Feeling more relaxed, I paid attention to the thoughtful pretty paper and ribbons that wrapped our presents. Although I had found the gifts Mom and Dad had bought, I didn't know who was getting what. I was worried I was getting the chemistry set.

My Christmas tradition was to wake up in the middle of the night when everybody else was asleep to check the tags on our presents. By the time I saw our presents under the tree; Santa had already been to our house. I'd spend a half-hour or so reading the different gift tags and feeling the gifts through the wrapping paper. I tried to remember the various gifts I had found so I'd know what Joey and I were getting before we opened our gifts about 6 in the morning. A couple of times I thought about changing the gift tags if Joey was getting something I wanted but I figured I'd get caught. He'd let me use his stuff anyway.

This year was more challenging to figure out who was getting what by feeling through the wrapping paper to the packages. The presents I found this year were different than previous years. There weren't any cowboy or soldier toy guns. Instead, I found a game called Risk and a game called Stratego. I couldn't figure out who was getting which game by the feel of the packages. I had found a plastic statue of Stan Musial which I prayed was for me, and a silver-monogrammed name bracelet that was for Joey. I was disappointed to see so many dress shirts, ties and pants. In my search through the treasure, I realized this was the biggest haul Joey and I had ever received. It was probably due to his illness.

There were several large wrapped boxes behind the tree I had never found during my searches. How had I missed them? I scurried like a rat to find some clue. They were tagged to Joey and me and they felt somewhat heavy. They were too big to shake in their box. Where and how had Mom and Dad hidden them from me? I decided not to unwrap the boxes in case I tore the wrapping paper.

I crawled back to the couch and laid down while I stared at the mysterious gifts wondering, between yawns, what they were.

My power of concentration was fuzzy. I was tired, and it was well past two in the morning when I fell asleep.

Shocked awake, my heart was racing like a bunny rabbit's when I felt Dad shaking my shoulder and whispering in my ear.

"Wake up, Mickey. Wake up. I hear him. Did you see him? Was he here? Did you get a photo of him?"

"What? What? Who, Dad?"

"Are you kidding me? Santa that's who."

"No, I didn't. I must've fallen asleep," I mumbled, crestfallen.

"Hurry, get up. Let's go outside, Mickey. We might still be able to see him or his sleigh and reindeers. Hurry!" Dad tugged on my arm, pulled me off the couch and bum-rushed me up the basement stairs and out the front door of our house.

It was a fairy-tale-like scene. The colored Christmas lights on everyone's homes were reflecting off the brilliant falling white snow lit by the almost full Yule Moon overhead. Snow? Wait a minute, what happened? Overnight, it must've started snowing. It looked like we had about three inches, and it was still coming down hard. We were having a white Christmas!

"Quiet, Mickey. Listen. What do you hear? Do you hear any jingle bells or anything?"

It was a silent night. It was the quietest moment I had ever heard. I could actually hear the snow falling and landing and then it hit me.

"Yeeoww, Dad, my feet are freezing," I screeched splitting the silence of the night. My teeth were chattering too.

"Quiet, Mickey. This might be our last chance to see Santa. Didn't you wear your slippers?" he whispered, looking at my bare feet. His slippers were on his feet.

"No, we just rushed out of the house," I whimpered while I shivered and climbed onto the top of his slippers.

"Darn. Let's try to hear Santa one more time," he said as we huddled closer together. "Do you hear Santa, Mickey?"

"I'm not sure, maybe, way off in the distance. Yeah, I think I do."

"I think I do too, Mickey. Let's go inside."

Once inside, everyone was awake and my teeth were chattering non-stop. Mom had towels and socks to dry and warm our feet as Joey came up from the rathskeller.

"Well, the jolly old elf was here," he said with a twinkle in his eye. "What did he look like, Mickey? Did he look like the Santa in the Coca-Cola ads?"

"How do you know he was here, Joey?"

"Duh, he left presents downstairs, and he ate the Swiss cheese you left out for him."

"I didn't see him. I fell asleep," I said dejectedly hiding the secret I had eaten the cheese. "Dad woke me when he heard him, and we went outside but we didn't see him. We might've heard him though. Right, Dad?" I said, shaking my head, yes.

"Yeah, I'm pretty sure I heard him," said Dad nodding agreement.

"You must've taken his picture, Mickey. Look!" said Joey holding up and pointing to the Kodak Instamatic. "The flashbulb is melted. Somebody sure took a photo."

Joey was right. Someone had taken a color photo with the Instamatic. Had Santa taken a picture of himself? I was beyond excited, and I planned to rush the film to Rexall's to get it developed after Christmas. I'd see it in a week or so, and then nobody could argue with me about Santa anymore.

"I have an idea," proclaimed Grandma. "Since we're already up and awake, let's make some hot chocolate and open our presents right now. Okay?"

It didn't take any effort to convince everybody. We were all wide-awake, and although my feet were cold they weren't numb anymore. Besides, I remembered those boxes downstairs, and my curiosity was tearing at me.

❧

CHAPTER 12

WONDERFUL CHRISTMASTIME

om didn't need another miracle to get us to Mass; even if there were five inches of snow covering everything. All she needed was Joey and me shoveling our sidewalk and driveway, and Dad driving the stick transmission through the snow to church. She never even considered skipping Mass especially after receiving a bona fide Christmas Miracle.

We were tired but thrilled we were all together. We'd stayed up most of the night opening presents, eating treats, drinking hot chocolate and talking about almost catching Santa. We were powered by adrenalin and Mom's deep devotion following her miraculous apparition.

My favorite part, if there was one for a kid, about going to Mass during Advent was seeing the Nativity Scene set up in church. It made God more real, and the story of being born in a stable made Jesus relatable. It's not that I was born in a barn but I lived in a world of make-believe. I imagined the detailed foot-tall figurines of kings, shepherds and baby Jesus were real. The exotic camels were especially cool.

Most of the parents in church looked exhausted. They had circles as big as Christmas wreaths under their eyes. The weather didn't stop the kids from dressing in their new Christmas clothes along with their warmest winter coats, scarves, hats, gloves and boots. We were all happy to be praying together again. Like the painted sign in Old English letters above the church door said, "A family that prays together, stays together."

Father kept Mass moving along. There were lots of crying babies and young kids with visions of sugarplums and new toys that needed attention. My head reeled from thinking about my possible encounter with Santa. I planned to sell my photo of Santa and buy everything I ever thought about wanting for Christmas.

Half asleep and in a dream state, Mass was a blur of Latin, singing, standing, sitting and kneeling. I remembered to say short prayers of thanks for Joey's recovery and all of the great gifts.

Groggy and not paying much attention, I was hit in the back of the head with a snowball Larry threw on the way to our car. "Merry Christmas, Mickey Mouse," he yelled as he ducked my return volley but he got hit by Tommy's rocket-fast snowball to the back.

"Nice shot, Tommy! I'll meet you guys at Heart Attack Hill after lunch to go sled riding," I yelled.

"What'd you get for Christmas, Mickey?" asked Tommy.

"I got a catcher's mitt, a portable stereo record player and the Beatles' album," I shouted safely hiding behind a parked car.

"What'd you get?" I asked as I prepared a snowball for a head-shot when Larry peaked around a car.

"I got a record player and a new sleeping bag," said Tommy as my snowball sailed wide of Larry and hit the side of a car.

"Cool, see you guys later," I said as I crawled into the back seat as a flurry of snowballs hit the side of our car.

It was going to be a busy day but the first thing we needed was a good nap and that was where we found ourselves—flat on our backs. We were worn-out.

We had resting bodies everywhere. We were lying on the couch, in our beds and I was on the floor under the tree. Grandma just wanted to "rest my eyes a minute," so she sat up in an easy chair. She had a quiet, swishing snore so quiet you couldn't actually hear it. After two hours and still a little bleary, Joey and I got dressed to go outside and slide on our sleds down Heart Attack Hill.

Snow on Christmas Day was a rare gift in the City of Saints. It had only happened once before that I could remember. Usually, our cold, snowless, brown grass Christmas days were spent visiting friends' houses to eat cookies and play with presents. After seeing what everyone got and comparing your Christmas haul to theirs, we'd circle back home for our traditional baked ham dinner. As we got older, our friends would come over to play board games.

This Christmas was different. We had a perfect snowfall. It was a great present that nobody expected. There was plenty of snow and it was a little wet, so it packed perfectly for snowballs and sledding. Since the temperature was below freezing, we knew the snow was going to last a while but we didn't intend to waste our once-in-a-decade opportunity.

We lived in a blue-collar neighborhood. Nobody in our neighborhood traveled to Colorado or Idaho for winter ski vacations. Heck, I had never even seen the Rockies, much less a pair of skis, except in the movies. Our friends' dads were mailmen, machinists, bus drivers, barbers, engineers, plumbers, carpenters, salesmen, office and government workers. Only a few of our mothers worked out of our homes. Winter sledding was our winter vacation, and we weren't going to squander it. We would sled on any field, street or parking lot as long as there was a hill and it had more snow or ice than mud or gravel.

This was the first snowfall of the year. We had gotten our sleds ready in October—just in case. We took the art of sledding fast and reckless downhill, seriously.

Men have grown up dreaming about going faster ever since the beginning of time. Why do you think men invented the wheel from a rock? Simple, it gave us two things. Speed and rock and roll. Before boys made vroom vroom sounds to imitate a combustion engine or put baseball cards in the spokes of their bikes to imitate motorcycle sounds, they made the clomp-clomp sounds of a running horse by drumming on the nearest hard surface including tables, chests, and heads. That's why Streak was every kid's, and many men's, hero. He built cars that went fast, unusually fast. It wasn't enough for our sleds to get down a snowy hill. They had to get down the hill—fast.

Joey and I inherited an American Flexible Flyer and a Champion F47 sled from Dad and his older brother. The sleds needed care but they were sturdy, fast and agile. With Dad's help, we counter-screwed the weathered boards onto the frames so the boards wouldn't come off or rip our clothes. We also tied new pull ropes onto the steering handles.

This year we tried something new to go faster. First, we honed the metal runners with sandpaper and steel wool to remove any paint, rust and uneven surfaces. Next, we coated the sleds' steel runners with melted candle wax to create a coating to go faster. We got the idea on a sliding board at summer camp last summer.

After going down the tall sliding board a couple of times, the guys got bored. It was too slow. We barely made it down the slide, and at the end of it, we had to skootch on our butts to get off. We tried all kinds of things to go faster. Nothing worked until we sat on the waxed paper our moms used to wrap our sandwiches. Eureka! We sped down so quickly seated on the waxed paper that we'd fly off the end of the sliding board.

Heart Attack Hill got its name because some man, who must've been a scaredy-cat, had a heart attack going down the hill. By the time we arrived there, about a dozen guys were racing down it. Heart Attack was steep, and it had some natural obstacles like rocks and trees on the way down, which made it challenging. Its biggest obstacle was a very narrow passage we called Fat Man's Squeeze about three-quarters of the way down. The Squeeze was lined with trees on the left side and a twenty-foot steep hill on the other. More than one guy ran into one of the trees or went over the edge and had gotten hurt.

Sledding at Heart Attack Hill was perfect for adrenalin junkies too poor to ski and too young to drive, fly or skydive. Having the frigid, snowy wind slap you in the face as you soared down a snowy hillside eight inches off the ground was exhilarating. The faster we flew, the faster we wanted to fly. It's how many boys, and some girls, are wired. Being on the edge between fear and exhilaration created a palpable reaction. Your stomach felt like you ate your heart.

There were lots of ways to ride down a hill on a sled, and we've tried them all. The basic method is to sit on your sled, use the rope like reins, and steer with your feet on the steering bar. You need someone to push you or you'll have a tough time getting started. It's not very fast because it's such a slow way to start. You can also lay on your sled and steer with your hands but you still need someone's help to get started.

The fastest way to ride a sled down a hill required speed, agility, and balance. You started about 10 yards or more from the starting line holding your sled across your chest by its side rails. Then, you made a mad dash to the starting line and slung your sled down in front of you towards the ground without letting go. At the last moment, you belly-flopped onto the sled's wooden deck just as the sled hit the ground. After landing, you immediately grabbed the steering bar or you swerved and lost your fast start. You got a little extra speed if you pumped your legs as you sped down the hillside.

As Joey and I trudged up the long hill, we stopped about halfway to let him catch his breath. It was easy to see he wasn't himself yet. He was tired.

"Are you okay, Joey?"

"Yeah, I'm fine. I'm just out of shape. I was lying in that hospital bed for a month. It makes me tired to even walk."

"Your legs don't hurt do they, Joey?" I hadn't stopped worrying about him.

"Yeah, you better be worried because I'm going to beat you down this hill all day long, Mickey," he laughed and started slogging up the hill again.

Once we got to the top, all of the guys rushed over to say hello, clap Joey on the back and find out what happened. Life was normal again, and I wasn't worried about my brother dying. It felt great to have us all together again and to have a hill full of snow on Christmas to keep us busy. With the guys stopping to shoot the breeze and catch up, it was easy for Joey to sit on his sled and avoid sledding down and walking up the hill.

The guys were taking turns riding down the hill doing all of the crazy stuff they could think of doing. Sledding was dangerous. Lots of things could go wrong when someone tried to go too fast on icy surfaces. Last year, we had an ice storm and thought it would be fun to do some ice sledding. It was but as Dad always said, "It's all fun until somebody gets hurt." My footing slipped on the ice and I missed my belly flop. The left side of my face scraped along the ice for a few feet and bled until Mom bandaged me up.

Fortunately, we were young show-offs. Fear never stopped us from doing dumb or goofy things. Have you ever tried to stand on a sled and ride down a hill holding the rope? Don't. Your feet are going to slide off the front, and you're going to get hurt. It was pretty standard for people to fall off their sleds, and get run over by someone not watching or being unable to react.

Today, we were seeing how many guys we could stack up on a sled, and still race down the hill. We stacked three guys on a sled when we laid on top of each other. We didn't quite make it to Fat Man's Squeeze before the sleds crashed into each other. It was impossible to steer.

We got even higher, but not as far, when we built a pyramid with 10 guys, using four sleds abreast. It was a spectacular crash. We also made sled trains with guys having snowball fights all of the way down the hill. The trains usually ended up in a tangle of sleds and laughing bodies.

There were as many ideas about how to sled down a snowy hillside as there were guys. One time, I saw a group of guys unbolt the hood of their Ford Galaxy and pack six guys on it. They slid down Art Hill, crashing onto the lagoon ice sending everyone into the freezing water. Everybody clapped as their friends rushed to pull everyone out of the water.

We built a ramp in the middle of the hill to add some daredevil thrills and stunts. It took a while to make it because we only had the one snow shovel Billy brought. Each guy took his turn and hauled snow shovel full by shovel full. We didn't really get it too high in the air, but it felt like we were 50 feet off the ground.

Throwing snowballs at guys while they were sledding went together like Coke and chipped ice. We aimed for the body but occasionally someone caught one with his face, which hurt and generally made somebody mad.

Stubby, the class clown, had the best Hollywood crash so far today. He didn't mean for it to happen. He sat down on his sled backward and had us push him to get started. It didn't take us long to realize his trajectory was off. He was heading straight towards the trees at the Squeeze. As we watched the accident unfold in real time, we waved and yelled at Stubby about the trees. He didn't realize what was happening and he couldn't hear us.

He was doing all of his Curly head slaps and hand waves back at us until his sled crashed head-on into a maple tree which didn't move. Stubby did a backward roll up the trunk of the tree until he was doing a headstand on his sled. It was terrifying and hilarious at the same time. We knew it hurt because several of the guys who went down to help him had to walk him home. Except for a few injuries, none of which required stitches or a hospital, it was the most fun afternoon I could remember since the farm.

There were two ways to know when it was time to go home when we were outside playing in the snow. The first was when our parents told us to be home at a particular time, or we'd get grounded. The second was when our feet, hands and in some cases our faces were so numb from the cold we couldn't feel them. As the snow melted through our clothes and touched our skin, and as the temperature dropped, it was painful until that part of our bodies got numb.

None of us had waterproof clothes and only a few of us had waterproof shoes or boots. It wasn't strange to see guys sledding in tennis shoes or old dress shoes. Many of us had hand-me-down coats, hats, pants, gloves and boots.

We tried different ideas to keep our feet dry and warm. We had outgrown the black rubber boots that we slipped over our regular shoes when we were kids. Only a few of us had water-proofed brown suede lace-up boots we called "boondockers." We wore as many pairs of socks as we could fit under our boots and shoes. Once, we tried wrapping our feet in bread wrappers to keep them dry, but that didn't work. They made our feet sweat and get even colder.

The colder we got, the less sledding we did. Before long we were all sitting at the top of Heart Attack Hill talking trash. Our hands and feet were numb, and the sun was beginning to set. Everybody was bragging about their Christmas presents when Billy asked the question.

"Hey Suzie, did Santa come to your house this year?" Everyone laughed but me.

"Yeah, he did Billy, and he told me you were a big jerk," I said as I flipped some snow into his face.

"Hey punk, what're you doing?" laughed Billy as Dave hit him with a snowball in the back of his head.

"Hey Dave, stop, or you're going to get hurt."

"Oh, are you going to get your big sister to help you, Billy?" chided Dave, as Tommy dropped a giant clump of snow over Dave's head and Rusty said, "Dave's going to kill you, Tommy."

"Ooh, I'm scared," said Tommy shaking his hands, as Henry pushed him over Larry, who was kneeling behind Tommy. Everybody laughed.

"Why don't you guys grow up and act like men," said Johnny as he stood up and farted by Hank's head.

"What the heck?" said Hank as he farted at no one in particular and said, "I guess Joey and I are the only grown-ups here."

"I'm a grown-up," said Greg as he walked behind Charlie and stuck a snowball down the neck of his coat.

"What're you doing? The snow's cold," cried Charlie as he tore frantically at his coat to remove the snow. Dave shoved snow down the back of Greg's pants.

"Dave, you better run," warned Greg.

"Why? You can't catch me," crowed Dave, as Kevin and Denny slung snowballs that hit Billy on either side of his head.

Everyone was pointing and laughing at Greg saying, he had snowman poop down his pants as he reached down his pants to pull the snow out. 'You'll get yours," is all he could say as he shivered.

"I've got to get home for dinner," said Johnny. "Hey Joey, let's get together to practice with our new electric guitars this week. They each got one for Christmas.

"You guys should start a rock and roll band," I suggested.

"Great idea, Suzie, you can be their Go-Go dancer," laughed Billy as two more snowballs from Denny and Kevin hit him in the chest. They just laughed.

"Stop throwing snowballs at me, you guys," said Billy getting serious as one flew just a little over his head, and another hit him in the stomach. "I mean it," he threatened. They each made another snowball.

"I've got an idea," said Ed pointing his gloved hand high into the air as if he just invented electricity.

"That's impossible. You have to have a brain to think of an idea," said Jim, who pushed Kurt into John as they both fell down.

"Listen you guys. Let's have one last gigantic race down Heart Attack Hill. Everybody races at the same time." Then, in his best Wrestling at the Chase announcer voice, Ed said, "It's a winner takes all, no-holds-barred race. You can do anything you want to other guys to stop them from winning. The first guy to pass the lamp post at the bottom of the hill wins."

We all enthusiastically agreed and started shaking our heads up and down while threatening the others and bragging. Then, we picked up our sleds and walked over to where Ed was starting the race.

Lots of taunts, jeers and snowballs were passed back and forth as we stood ready to run and flop on our sleds.

"On your mark, get set, go!" screamed Ed. We picked up our sleds and took off running towards the edge of the long descent down Heart Attack Hill. At the starting line, only one guy flopped on his sled and headed down the now well-worn icy fast hill, Joey.

The rest of us just stood and watched him slide down over the ramp past the Squeeze and finally past the lamp post. It was the only time Joey sledded all day. No one wanted to take a chance of hurting him. We knew he wasn't totally well. He was still mending, yet, Joey won the Christmas Day race.

Then, one by one, we took our last Christmas Day ride, together.

"Geez, that was a dirty trick," Joey mock yelled at us. "I can't believe I missed you guys when I was in the hospital."

Everybody laughed and went their separate ways to eat dinner.

Joey and I walked together pulling our sleds in the silence of the night. There were only a few stars and the Yule moon lighting our way. We kept to our own thoughts.

I was trying to understand why I wanted to cry and laugh at the same time.

I had grown up a lot this past year. I even made enough money to buy everyone's Christmas gift. It seemed like a lifetime ago when we were kids goofing off in the creek and sewers and playing baseball. I barely knew who the Beatles were then, and now they were my favorite group. I had their album and longer hair. Who cared about Elvis?

We didn't take anything too seriously last summer unless it had a two-cent deposit. Then, our friend Allen died and then President Kennedy. They were too young, and I was terrified when Joey got sick and went to the hospital.

Last summer, I wasn't really sure I believed in God, but I believed in Santa. Now, well you get the idea, I'm growing up in the City of Saints.

Q & A INTERVIEW WITH DENNIS GANAHL

Author's Background

Writing my first novel wasn't intimidating because I wasn't smart enough to be afraid. Writing my second novel was frightening. I remember thinking, 'Anybody can write one book but if you can't write a second you're not really an author.' After my second novel, I'm confident, there'll be a third.

I loved growing up in the 1950s and 60s in a new Catholic suburb where all of our streets were named after saints and full of kids. St. Ann was primarily a blue-collar town with some white-collar government and office workers sprinkled around. Our mothers made sure their homes were tidy, and most of our fathers worked on their own cars and homes. Kids knew they were supposed to be seen but not heard if parents were around. So, the best plan was not to be seen. Kids weren't given a choice about being good. They were expected to work hard enough to get into heaven.

There wasn't much privacy in our small homes or in our neighborhoods. We knew our neighbors' names and we called the adults Mr. or Mrs. People argued with their windows open in the summer because it was just too darn hot to close them. We didn't have wash and wear clothing. Nobody ironed their blue jeans but everybody ironed their clothes for work and church. Some people thought they were better than others but they weren't because everybody, except older people, cut their own grass. Most of the kids loved their parents and their country.

I was blessed to grow up in a time and place when everything, and everyone, moved slower. Our escalators noisily rumbled instead silently sweeping us to the next floor. Elevators had actual operators that smiled. Today, some cars don't have drivers, and we don't talk to a telephone operator. Life has become sleek and, in my mind, less romantic. *Scouts & Scalawags*, like *Heroes & Hooligans*, will give you a safe refuge from the nanosecond speed of the world.

Why did you choose 1963 and St. Ann, Missouri for the setting of your humorous historical fiction novel?

They are an era and place that literature has overlooked. The Midwest's values and lifestyles have interested the world since Mark Twain and Laura Ingalls Wilder wrote about them in the 1800s. Walt Disney, another Midwesterner, carried the Midwest's values around the globe with lovable heroes like the innocent Mickey Mouse and the Midwest's Main Street lifestyle at Disney World. Like the Mississippi river town Hannibal was for the 1800s, St. Ann was emblematic of America's post-war suburban Boomer lifestyle.

In America, 1963 was a landmark year that violently ended a period of relative calm, and it kicked-off a tumultuous era. The Civil Rights movement, Women's Rights and the Vietnam War were all escalating. The Catholic Church was turning upside down with Vatican II's birth and Pope John XXIII's death. We also were dealing with the assassinations of Medgar Evers, President Kennedy and Lee Harvey Oswald. Pop culture was changing from Andy Griffith to James Bond.

Who are your aspiring authors?

Mark Twain is my pinnacle because of his adventurous and humorous stories about early life in Missouri. I also enjoy Laura Ingalls Wilder in particular for her attention to the historical facets of life on the plains. I laugh out loud watching Jean Shepherd's Christmas Story and reading his writings.

What is the scope of your storyline?

Heroes & Hooligans Growing Up in the City of Saints is the first part, and *Scouts & Scalawags Growing Up in the City of Saints* is the second part of a historical fiction coming-of-age saga in 1963. The novels follow the Catholic liturgical year. The books begin with Easter and end on Christmas day.

What kind of reactions have you received to your book?

My books are written to make readers feel nostalgic and warm inside. Many readers assume my novels are based on true stories because of the level of detail I use to tell my stories. I remind people the stories are fictional and so are the characters. They keep thinking I'm Mickey. I provide historically accurate context when

I describe the characters and their families, values, lifestyle, food and activities. Almost everyone who reads my books, no matter their age, say they did the same things growing up as Mickey and his friends.

Critical review quote:

Mary Troy, literature professor at the University of Missouri St. Louis and author of *Beauties*, winner of the USA Book Award; said about *Heroes & Hooligans*, "the humor is organic and not contrived…the narrator gives a mature perspective to the story.

I enjoyed it."

LITERATURE NERD'S FUN FACTS ABOUT GROWING UP IN THE CITY OF SAINTS

Setting

St. Ann is an *Integral Setting* that illuminates the characters and updates the rich historical Midwest of Twain and Wilder. Like Tom, Huck, Laura, Mary and Carrie from the 1800s, Mickey and his friends are Midwest kids living in 1963.

Themes

The *Explicit* theme of good behavior versus bad is described in the title of the book and its opening sentence. There are multiple *Implicit* themes used throughout the book like friendship, masculinity, morality, courage and religion.

Plot

The books are written in *Chronological Order* and each chapter has its own *Episodical plot. Flashbacks* are used to give perspective and depth to the characters and events of the moment being faced by Mickey and his friends.

The books use an assortment of protagonist conflicts including *Person-against-self, Person-against-person* and the soulful duel, *Person-against-religion.*

Mickey, the *Protagonist,* is a fourth and then fifth-grade Catholic living in a suburban Catholic mecca. Mickey's in constant personal conflict because he's unable to satisfy everyone's expectations and his own at the same time.

Writing Style

The author uses narrator *Exposition* and character *Dialogue* styles for telling the stories. To provide a complete sensory reading experience, the books use lavish word play to develop imagery, figures of speech from 1963, similes, metaphors, hyperbole, and symbols. To complete the auditory adventure, the stories contain *Onomatopoeia*, *Alliteration*, *Assonance*, *Consonance* and *Rhythm* and *Rhyme*. There are two music stations on Spotify to replicate the 1963 AM radio station soundscape.

Point-of-view

The books rely on Mickey's *First-Person* point of view.

Tone

The books were written to be humorous and sentimental. There are chapters which teach the boys serious, moral and mortal lessons.

Character development

The novel has *Round Characters* with values, attitudes and beliefs that are developed through speech, appearance, actions and retrospective self-talk and reflection.

Pattern-of Action

Using strategic foreshadowing, each chapter uses *Rising Action* that builds to *Climax* and *Resolution* by the end of the chapter. Each chapter chronicles Mickey's journey to grow up and the last chapter brings the books to a close.

These are some of the readers' quotes from Amazon reviews about *Heroes & Hooligans Growing Up in the City of Saints*. Heroes & Hooligans is the first book of the Growing Up in the City of Saints series. Scouts & Scalawags continues the story of the boys growing up.

"What a fun collection of stories about growing up! Boys are such a funny breed - one minute completely crazy and the next completely sweet. These stories bring both sides to light and are a reminder that even the most rambunctious boys have huge and beautiful hearts." Hadley Barrows, author

"A great look at growing up Catholic in the 60s. The characters' voices ring true and reflect a simpler time when bicycles and families meant everything. Ganahl has snapped a picture of a life we will never see again." Bill Klutho

"It's a hoot! Especially the so true stories about the Catholic Nuns! God love 'em." Alfred Tuchfarber, author

"Great book. Easy read. Lots of funny stories that will immediately transport you to the magical life of childhood. Thanks, and write another one!" Joe

"I loved this book! It is the most enjoyable book that I've read in years. The character development was so well done that you really care about each character in the story. I'd recommend this book to everyone whether you grew up in the Midwest or not." Tina Odo

"Boomer magic. Boomers will laugh at how relatable it is and Boomers' children will now understand their parents. Fun read." –Diane Schumacker

"His book brought back sweet memories of people and places I haven't thought of in a very long time. Dennis has a knack of writing from within a young boy's mind and heart, sharing his thoughts, emotions, and secrets." –Bonnie Pratt Hutton

"Great book! Written by a witty and creative storyteller writer. I could have sworn I was the main character! –Urzlavo

"It was a great read. Many of the stories reminded me of events from my childhood. Dennis has a wonderful story-telling style that you will enjoy as well." –Larry Porschen

"It doesn't matter if you grew up in St. Louis. What I really enjoyed was that each chapter captured a specific life experience that shaped the development of Mickey, while the author describes life's lessons. A fun read!" –Jaime Correa

"Ganahl's book brought back many happy childhood memories. The book was filled with fun and suspense. You will keep wanting to look ahead. Resist the temptation as there are many surprises along the way." –Paul Grew

"You fall in love with the cast of witty, complex characters. There's so much more than meets the eye at first glance with this book. I couldn't put it down. Do yourself a favor, read this book!" –Amazon Customer

"A wonderful tapestry of life stories in the 60's in St. Louis! The collection of stories makes you smile, laugh, and reminisce about simpler times. It doesn't matter in which part of St. Louis you grew up; you can remember similar people, places, and happenings. The book leaves you wanting more stories!" –Anonymous

Get your printed and electronic copies of *Heroes & Hooligans* and *Scouts & Scalawags Growing Up in the City of Saints*. Simply go online and order yours from Amazon and Kindle. Thanks!